"Hey, don't do that!"

Ali turned and saw Jack standing, his books scattering to the floor.

"What—?"

Her words were cut off by a low, explosive sound and a burst of energy whizzing past her. A mirror on the far side of the room shattered, and Jack was shouting, "Down, get down! Now!"

He tackled her, jerking her down to the floor, and literally covered her body with his. For a heartbeat she was lost in heat and silence and a sense of security she'd never known in her life before. Then Jack drew back just enough to look at her.

She could feel tension trembling in his arms, his heart hammering against her breasts. "Are you all right?" he asked.

"Someone . . . shot at us?"

"Us? *You,* Miss Sullivan. Someone shot at *you.*"

Dear Reader,

The New Year is starting off splendidly here at Silhouette Intimate Moments. Take our American Hero, for instance. Riley Cooper, in Marilyn Pappano's *No Retreat,* is a soldier with a soft side. When his first love walks back into his life, troublemaking son in tow, it's surrender time for this tough guy.

Laurey Bright, long a favorite with readers of the Silhouette Special Edition line, makes her first Intimate Moments novel a winner. In *Summers Past* you'll find passion, betrayal and one all-important question: Who *is* little Carley's father? Allyson Ryan's *Secrets of Magnolia House* takes a few spooky detours along the road to romance; I think you'll enjoy the ride. *Two for the Road* is the first of Mary Anne Wilson's new "Sister, Sister" duo; look for *Two Against the World,* coming soon. Joanna Marks lights up the night with *Heat of the Moment,* and Justine Davis checks in with *Race Against Time,* a tale full of secrets, crackerjack suspense and irresistible desire. In short—I don't think you'll want to miss a single one of this month's books.

As the year goes on, look for books by more of your favorite authors. Kathleen Eagle, Doreen Roberts, Paula Detmer Riggs and Marilyn Pappano are only a few of the great writers who'll be coming your way in Silhouette Intimate Moments. And then there's our Tenth Anniversary celebration in May! Be sure to join us for all the fun.

Leslie Wainger
Senior Editor and Editorial Coordinator

TWO FOR THE ROAD

Mary Anne Wilson

Published by Silhouette Books New York

America's Publisher of Contemporary Romance

SILHOUETTE BOOKS
300 East 42nd St., New York, N.Y. 10017

TWO FOR THE ROAD

ISBN: 0-373-07472-7

First Silhouette Books printing January 1993

All the characters in this book have no existence
outside the imagination of the author and have
no relation whatsoever to anyone bearing the same
name or names. They are not even distantly
inspired by any individual known or unknown
to the author, and all incidents are pure invention.

®: Trademark used under license and
registered in the United States Patent and
Trademark Office and in other countries.

Printed in the U.S.A.

Books by Mary Anne Wilson

Silhouette Intimate Moments

MARY ANNE WILSON

fell in love with reading at age ten when she discovered *Pride and Prejudice*. A year later she knew she had to be a writer when she found herself writing a new ending for *A Tale of Two Cities*. A true romantic, she had Sydney Carton rescued, and he lived happily ever after.

Though she's a native of Canada, she now lives in California with her husband and three children, a six-toed black cat who believes he's Hungarian and five timid Dobermans, who welcome any and all strangers. And she's writing happy endings for her own books.

For Amy, Tim and the newest Levin—
Taylor Anne
With all my love

Prologue

Alison Sullivan wasn't too sure just what the inside of a police station was supposed to look like. She'd seen them on television, but until an hour ago, she'd never been through the doors of one.

Now she knew that a station in the greater Los Angeles area wasn't any garden spot, with little warmth and even less decorating style. The building was four stories high, made of stone and brick outside. Inside it was starkly utilitarian, with pale green walls, brown tile floors, fake-wood desks, hard chairs and a steady drone of noise hanging in air that smelled strangely of disinfectant and stale cigarettes.

An hour ago, Sergeant Lewis, a big man with a bushy mustache and gray-streaked hair, had taken Ali to the second floor and put her into an interrogation room, an enclosed cubicle off the main squad room.

Then he'd left, and no one had been in to see her or talk to her since.

She'd memorized the room. No two-way mirrors, no rubber hoses, just a plain wooden table, which had its share of obscene words and random numbers carved into its top, and four chairs. Nothing was on the green walls except a Just Say No To Drugs banner in red, white and blue, and a plain clock bolted to the wall.

Midnight.

Ali sat stiffly in the straight-backed chair, her stomach in such knots she felt sick. She should have said no to her sister. She should have refused to take part in anything her sister thought up. She closed her eyes, then exhaled. What was Lydia going to say? Ali knew they'd called her foster mother as soon as Sergeant Lewis had brought her in, and she hated to face Lydia and tell her what she'd done.

She jumped when she heard a loud crash out in the hall, then the door was flung open and Alicia came stumbling into the room. Sergeant Lewis was right behind her, his hand in the middle of her back propelling her forward.

"I don't know what in the hell you're up to, but I'll be damned if you'll run around these halls as if you own the place." He slammed the door shut, then turned, his face dark with anger.

"This is police brutality," Alicia said, squaring herself to face the man.

But Lewis wasn't looking at her any longer. He saw Ali at the table, and his mouth went slack with shock. His eyes darted back to Alicia, who was standing in front of the table, tugging at the pink sweater she was wearing with her jeans, the same clothes Ali was wearing.

Lewis looked back to Ali. And Ali could almost see him thinking—red curly hair tumbling around their shoulders, green eyes, heart-shaped faces, slender, tall. The same person. The only difference at the moment was Alicia's smile and Ali's frown.

He shook his head. "Okay, I give up. What's going on?"

Alicia calmly perched on the edge of the table and crossed her arms over her chest. "After the way you treated me? I want to know what you've been doing to my sister!"

Lewis's face darkened again, the veins in his neck bulging ominously. "Doing to your sister?" he spat out, his voice rising with each word. "Doing to your sister! Doing, my ass. Your sister and her boyfriend rammed into the back of my patrol car. They caved in the whole damn trunk and punctured one of the tires."

Alicia looked at Ali, one finely arched eyebrow lifting, and a smile tugged at her pale lips. "Good heavens, sister dear, I asked you to go out with Brad because I thought he was a regular bore, and now this man is telling me that you and Brad destroyed his police car?"

Ali didn't share her humor at all. She'd agreed to take Alicia's place—not letting Brad know it—and get her sister out of a date she didn't want so she could go on one she'd waited for forever. She hadn't agreed to be put in jail because Brad turned out to be a jerk who had the car stocked with beer and who drove like a madman.

Ali sat forward, her hands pressed to the tabletop. "This isn't funny, *sister dear,*" she ground out. "My God, Brad hit Sergeant Lewis's car. And it's a mess. There were broken beer bottles all over Brad's car. It smelled like a brewery, and Brad's car is ruined."

"Oh, don't look so worried. You didn't do anything wrong, did you?"

"Of course not."

"You weren't driving, were you?"

"No, but—"

"And you surely weren't drunk, were you?"

"Alicia, I never—"

"Forget about it." She waved her hand in imperious dismissal. "You're an innocent bystander. Brad can get himself out of this mess, and meanwhile, Lydia's here. She's signing papers and they'll let you go." Alicia looked at Sergeant Lewis, by the door. "Would you be kind enough to check and see if the papers are done?"

"Gladly," the man muttered, and left.

When the door shut, Ali stood and faced Alicia across the table, her palms still pressed to the scarred wooden top. "*Never* ask me to do something like this for you again. *Never!*"

Alicia's smile didn't falter. "What, you didn't have fun?"

"I hated it," Ali muttered.

"But it was exciting, wasn't it? I can see the color in your cheeks, the sparkle in your eyes."

And Ali could see the glow of excitement in Alicia's face. Her sister was loving every minute of this. "It sucked," she bit out.

"*But* you had fun. You did something you wouldn't have done yourself. And Brad's sort of cute, don't you think?"

"I think Brad's a jerk. I think you're crazy, and I want to know how we're going to be able to face anyone when this gets out. They'll put it in the papers, you know."

Alicia stood and twisted a lock of her brilliant hair around one finger. "What's that old saying? It doesn't matter what they say about you as long as they spell your name right?"

"I don't want my name in the papers, and I don't want to be in this police station. I just want to go home." She tugged at her sweater, wondering if a shower would take the smell of this place off her and her clothes. "Maybe I can get out of here before any reporters find out."

"Let me know how this all comes out," Alicia said.

Ali looked at her. "Let you know?"

The smile faded, replaced by an expression Ali didn't quite understand at first. "Let me know if you're a branded woman after this incident."

Ali went around the table to face her sister, her mirror image, yet as different from her as night was from day. "Alicia, this was your idea. I would never have gone out with Brad except—"

"I'm leaving, Ali," she said bluntly.

"What?"

"I'm out of here. I got through high school by the skin of my teeth, and I want a change of scenery."

Ali felt her heart sink. "What about Lydia?" she asked, but really wanted to ask, "What about me?"

"Lydia understands. I told her about this yesterday. I was just waiting for the right time to tell you."

"A police station is the 'right time'?"

"I think so."

"Where will you go?"

"Anywhere. I just want to move." She laughed, but the sound didn't have a lot of humor in it. "Hey, don't look so depressed. I'll be back. You can't get rid of me that easily. I'll come and visit you and Lydia." She waved a hand to take in the small interrogation room. "Without me, you won't be getting yourself into trouble. You'll stay out of jails like this."

Somehow Ali had known this day would come, the day when Alicia would run from her roots and responsibilities. She just hadn't believed it would be this soon. And she hadn't counted on feeling as if the main part of herself would be leaving with her sister. "Will you be able to stay out of trouble without me to stop your crazy impulses?" she asked, her voice faintly unsteady.

Alicia laughed, a sound that echoed off the dull green walls. "Life wouldn't be worth living without some excitement in it."

And Alicia couldn't live without excitement. That need was part of her. She didn't want to be tied down by routine or sameness or security or responsibility. The twins, orphaned at five and bounced from foster home to foster home until they were twelve and came to live with Lydia and Harry Barrows, had made Ali value everything that Alicia wanted to turn her back on now. Ali held on to it for dear life. Alicia wouldn't take that chance and have it snatched away from her.

She'd walk away first. And Ali knew there was nothing she could say to stop Alicia from taking off.

"Is Lydia upset about all this?" Ali asked.

"Not really, although I think I heard her muttering something about being thankful 'dear, departed Harry' wasn't here to see this day—me leaving and you in jail."

"Alicia!"

Her sister slipped her arm through Ali's and started for the door with her. "Forget it. Let's go and find out if your Sergeant Lewis is going to let you go, or if I'm going to have to plan a jailbreak." She stopped at the door and looked at her twin. Her face sobered. "You know I'd do anything for you, don't you, Ali?"

"Yes," Ali said, "and I'd do anything for you."

Chapter 1

Ten Years Later
Los Angeles, Wednesday evening

Bad news always came at night, and when the phone rang just before midnight in the first week of October, Ali had the receiver in her hand after just two rings.

"Hello?" she said into the mouthpiece, her voice vaguely slurred with the remnants of sleep.

She expected to hear a doctor on the other end of the line, or maybe one of the special nurses taking care of her foster mother. But what she heard was the long-distance operator.

"Will you accept a collect call from Alicia?"

Ali scrambled to sit up in bed and groped for the light on the nightstand. "Yes, I'll accept," she said quickly. She'd been trying to contact her sister for three days, and this was the answer to her prayers. As she found the light and snapped it on, she heard, "Ali?"

The small light barely pushed back the shadows in the bedroom of the tiny California bungalow she shared with Lydia. Brushing the tangle of brilliant auburn hair off her face, she asked, "Where have you been, Alicia? I've been trying to call you since Sunday, and all I get is your answering machine."

"I haven't been at my apartment for a week," Alicia said, her voice barely audible.

For Alicia to drop out of sight wasn't anything new. It was a fact of life that Ali had accepted a long time ago. No strings, no bonds, nothing to hold Alicia down. Pick up and move whenever the mood struck her. Ali was just thankful that her sister had chosen to make one of her infrequent calls home tonight. "Alicia, I need to—"

But her sister cut her off with an unsteady whisper. "Ali, I'm in trouble."

Ali felt the words echo deep inside her, and she sank back against the wicker headboard of the double bed. Across the small shadowy room, she saw her image reflected back at her in the oval mirror hanging above the triple dresser.

She saw herself, but she never looked at herself without seeing her twin, the other half of who she was.

Both she and Alicia were tall; both had deep red hair that was wild with natural curl and fell well past their shoulders; both had true green eyes. But Ali had stayed with Lydia in the only home she'd known since her parents had died. Alicia had taken off right after high-school graduation. The last Ali had heard, her sister was a blackjack dealer in Las Vegas. Now she was talking about trouble.

"What kind of trouble, Alicia?" she asked, closing her eyes to shut out her reflection across the room.

She heard her sister take an unsteady breath before saying, "I met this man, and it turned out he's crazy."

A man. Ali began to ease a bit, to feel annoyance with her sister. "If you expect me to take some lunatic off your hands—"

"God, no, Ali. That's not why I'm calling." She hesitated, and the line hummed open for a moment before words spilled out. "He killed someone."

Ali's eyes flew open, and she could see herself in the mirror again, her face tinged with paleness. "Killed?" she managed.

"Murdered, and the police want me to testify against him." Her words were tumbling out in a shaky whisper. "They caught up with me last week, and they're holding me in protective custody. Ali, I don't know what to do."

Ali's stomach knotted with a vengeance. "What do you mean—you're supposed to testify?"

"They want me to testify in front of a grand jury so they can indict him for murder and hold him over for trial."

Ali pulled her knees to her chest and pressed her forehead against them. "Who is this person?"

"Mick Terrine. I thought he was just another customer in the casino, and he seemed so nice. He'd asked me out and we'd had drinks. Then one night, he asked me to have dinner, and when he met me, he had been drinking. He started rambling, telling me about something he'd done. Now the police say I'm the only one who can make sure he gets convicted for the murder.''

Ali felt numb. Since Lydia's heart attack three days ago, she'd felt as if she was walking through a nightmare. The idea of losing Lydia was staggering. She'd wanted to talk to Alicia about it, try to get her sister to come back to see their foster mother and give her some support, but now Ali didn't feel anything. It was as if she was sitting back looking down on life as an observer. She couldn't even speak.

Alicia didn't seem to notice her twin's lack of response. Words just kept tumbling out over words. ''They won't let me go. Monday I have to go to court and tell them what Mick said. I didn't want to call and worry you and Lydia, but I had to talk to someone. I feel like I'm going crazy.''

Lydia. Ali closed her eyes and swallowed hard as she was pulled back to reality and right into the middle of real fear. ''Alicia, that's why I was trying to call you. Lydia's in the hospital.''

''Oh, God, no,'' Alicia breathed.

''She's resting comfortably for now, but she's got a problem with her heart, a blockage of some sort. She has to have surgery on Tuesday. I've been trying to get hold of you. She wants you here, Alicia. She needs to see you.''

''Oh, Ali, if anything happens to her...''

Ali knew what Alicia was going to say. She felt the same way. Since Lydia and Harry had taken them in, Lydia had been their mother. She was all they had, besides each other. ''The doctor says he's optimistic about the operation. But she needs to see you, Alicia.''

"I need to see her, too, but I can't. The police won't let me step outside the door, let alone go to Los Angeles."

"Can't you tell the police what's happened? Surely they could bring you here or arrange something. It's an emergency. You aren't under arrest, are you?"

"No, not really, but I haven't told them about you and Lydia."

"Why not?"

"Mick Terrine isn't just anyone. His father's George Terrine, and he's really powerful around here. The police haven't even given my name out. They're keeping it all hush-hush until the grand jury convenes. Besides, if anyone knew about you and Lydia, they could use you to get to me."

"You don't think . . . ?"

"No, but they could put pressure on you or Lydia. They could threaten the two of you, and you know I'd do anything to keep you and Lydia safe. I can't take a chance of anyone knowing about my family."

Ali hugged her knees tightly with her arm. "I wish I could just get you and bring you here."

"So do I." Alicia was quiet for a moment, then spoke in a rushed whisper. "Is your hair still long?"

"What?"

"Is it?"

"Yes."

"Have you gained any weight?"

"I'm a hundred and fifteen pounds."

"It could work," Alicia whispered.

"What could work?"

"Listen. I can't talk much longer."

"Can you speak up, at least?"

"No, I have to keep my voice down. I had to pretend to be sick so I could get to the phone without the matron coming with me. Just listen so I don't have to repeat anything."

"All right."

"Remember Sergeant Lewis?"

Ali groaned softly. She'd never forget Sergeant Lewis. "Of course."

"Well, he thought I was you, and I bet he would have thought you were me, if he'd seen me first."

"Alicia, what are you talking about?"

"You could take my place here for the weekend, and I could come home and see Lydia."

"Oh, no," Ali said. "The last time we did that, I ended up in jail and you ended up leaving. No way. Besides, you said you're watched all the time. You couldn't possibly get away with anything like that. And, believe me, I don't think I could stand being in jail."

"I'm not in jail. They're keeping me in a hotel, a very nice hotel, and I have a single bodyguard. I think we could do it. We could change places."

"And we'd *both* end up in jail, or worse."

"Just hear me out."

Ali didn't think things could get any more confused or crazy. "Can I stop you?"

"No."

"Go ahead."

"This Friday afternoon I'm being taken downtown to the court building to meet with my attorney. They won't let him come here, and I've just found out that they're changing bodyguards at the same time. The matron who's been staying with me found out her daughter's having a baby, and she's going to leave."

Ali grasped at straws. "Couldn't this attorney help you get away from there legally?"

"He's a public defender and it's charity. He's sure not pulling down any big retainer giving me advice. I can't trust him." Alicia cut any rebuttal with a rush of whispered words. "The last time they took me to the court building, I used a bathroom on the bottom floor near a secured back entrance. I'll fake being sick on Friday, go to the rest room, and you be there. We can switch, and I'll fly back to L.A. and see Lydia at the hospital. Then I'll fly back and be there Monday morning and we can switch back the same way."

Ali felt her head spinning. "Alicia, you can't just walk into a rest room and have me walk out."

"Oh, damn it, here comes the matron. I don't have much more time. Please, do this for me. I have to see Lydia. What if something happens to her and I never get to see her again? All you have to do is be in that rest room at four o'clock on Friday, take my place, stay in a plush hotel room for the weekend and change back Monday."

Ali closed her eyes and wondered if she was as crazy as the world had become. But she knew how much it would mean to Lydia to see Alicia, and how much Alicia needed to see the only woman she remembered as her mother. She knew she'd regret it, but she found herself saying, "All right, I'll do it."

"Thanks," Alicia said in a rush. "Tell Lydia I'll be there to see her Friday night. And I'll see you in the rest room at four on Friday. Get in the last stall—it's the big one for the handicapped—and make sure no one can see your feet. Leave the door ajar. Oh, bring some money. I can't get to any. I have to go,'' she said quickly. "I love you." Then there was a click and the line buzzed.

Ali sat there for a long moment, then pushed the disconnect button without replacing the receiver. She dialed the number for the hospital, talked to the cardiac unit and found that Lydia was resting, that there was no change. Then she hung up and sat in the silence of her room.

How could things change so drastically in just a few days? She had a good life, a comfortable, pleasant life. And that was all she wanted. After a childhood of upheaval and uncertainty, she just wanted some peace and sameness.

Ali had worked at having a stable life. It meant everything to her. Just as freedom meant everything to Alicia. Now neither one had what they cherished.

Ali reached for the phone again, called the airline and made a reservation for a flight to Las Vegas on Friday morning, and a return flight under her name for eight o'clock that same evening. Then she reserved a flight from L.A. to Las Vegas at six-thirty in the morning on Monday, and a return flight to L.A. at noon.

After putting the phone back on the cradle, she slid down in the bed until she was lying with the covers pulled up to her chin. She stared into the shadows above her. She wouldn't tell Lydia about any of this. When Alicia got to see her, she could tell their foster mother as little or as much as she wanted to.

Ali had no one else to call, no one to tell she'd be away for a few days. She worked as a photographer with an advertising agency, and she made her own hours when the contracts came in. She was in a lull between jobs now, and her personal life had been in a lull for years. There wasn't anyone.

She occasionally dated a banker she'd met through the agency, but Roger Hann wasn't important to her. Unlike Alicia, who used to fall in and out of love at the drop of a hat, Ali didn't particularly believe in love. Of course, until a few minutes ago, she never would have believed her sister could have gotten mixed up with a man who was a murderer.

Ali closed her eyes and rolled onto her side, pulling her knees up to her stomach. How could all the old fear and sense of isolation come back so strongly—as if it had never been banished all those years ago?

Las Vegas—Thursday

Jackson Graham stared blindly at the tiny print in the law textbook, then finally sat back and closed his darkly lashed blue eyes. Words ran into words, ideas into ideas, and he was beginning to think that very little of what he had read in the past few weeks had made its way to his brain. He felt crammed and overloaded, but he knew he couldn't stop. He couldn't until he felt sure he'd be able to answer anything they threw at him when he took the state bar exam.

He tipped the chair back as he opened his eyes to the small side office on the second floor of the Las Vegas courthouse. The draperies behind him had been pulled to shut out the bright noonday sun that baked the sprawling city in sweltering heat. The air conditioner whirred in a soft steady drone, stirring the air with artificial coolness. Jack raked his fingers carelessly through sandy-blond hair that was overdue for a trim, then he sat forward, his chair thudding softly on the thick carpeting.

Resting his elbows on the cool wood of the desktop, he stared down at the open textbook. Was he fooling himself? Could he ever pass the exam, or was he just so anxious not to end up like every other cop he knew that he'd try anything to break out of the mold? A mold? Yes, that was exactly what he was in. With his father and two brothers both cops, and uncles and cousins involved in law enforcement, everyone said it was in his blood. He didn't have much choice. The Grahams were cops. Period.

But he didn't accept that. He'd gone to the police academy right out of college, then hired on with the Las Vegas P.D., but he'd never subscribed to living and dying a cop. Not like his father, and not like his brothers. He'd started law school, taking what courses he could while he worked full time. He ran a hand roughly over his face, and his fingers stilled on the well-healed scar that arched jaggedly across his chin.

Five years ago he'd stepped up his timetable. Nothing like facing death head-on to realize that life wasn't guaranteed, that any time you had on this earth was precarious at best.

He wanted to make sure that criminals paid for what they did, that they wouldn't walk away because of a technicality or a slipup in evidence or a failure to protect their rights. He wanted to sit behind the prosecutor's desk in court and convince a judge and jury that criminals shouldn't walk the streets.

He looked at the textbook with its pages of precedent rulings. He'd remember what he read. He'd know whatever he had to when he went in for the exam.

"Jack?"

He heard his name at the same moment he heard the door to the room thud back against the paneled wall. As Jack looked up, he saw Will Stanton, a barrel-chested balding man in a three-piece suit, his face pulled into an intense frown that seldom eased. Will had called this morning and asked Jack to meet him here. But Jack had no idea why.

He'd taken three weeks off work, using up his accumulated sick leave so he could study uninterrupted until next Wednesday. Jack closed the textbook and sat back in the swivel chair. "This had better be good."

Will shrugged out of his suit coat and hung it on a peg by the door. "I would have come by your place, but I didn't have the time, and . . ." He looked back at Jack, his eyes skimming over the worn jeans and blue T-shirt with the trademark of a sneaker company slashed across the chest. Then he looked at the law book. "You're really going to do it, aren't you?"

Jack was used to Will's cynicism about his ambitions. If anyone was a career cop, it was Will, and he was one of the best. "If I can remember what's in this book, I will." He spread his hand on its closed cover. "I wish I'd done this when I was younger, when my mind was more focused."

Will dropped down in the chair that faced the desk. "I hardly think you're approaching senility at thirty-five, but I've never figured why you wanted to get involved in this stuff, anyway. You know firsthand how frustrating it is to try and make sure justice is served."

"I'm just changing arenas, and being with the D.A. can't be any more frustrating than being behind a badge." Jack looked at Will. "And I won't have to shoot or be shot at." He drew his hand back and rested it on the coolness of the desktop. "Now that the philosophical questions are out of the way, why don't you tell me what you asked me down here for?"

"I need to ask you a favor," Will said without hesitating.

Jack was as close to Will as he was to anyone he'd ever worked with at LVPD, and almost as close as he was to either one of his brothers. "Anything. You can have my firstborn, although, the way my social life is going lately, you might have a very long wait." Jack spread both hands palms out to Will. "Or you can have all the money I have in my pocket at this moment, which is about ten bucks, give or take a quarter or two. The choice is yours."

"I appreciate the offers," Will said, his frown not easing at all. "I was actually thinking about something a bit more complicated, but less permanent."

Jack leaned back, rested one worn tennis shoe on the other knee and looked at Will through narrowed eyes. "Shoot."

"George Michael Terrine. Junior."

The name made Jack stop breathing for a second, and he slowly closed his hands over the wooden arms of the chair to keep himself from touching the scar on his chin. "What about Terrine?"

"You know I'm on the case, and you know you've been kept off of it."

"I noticed."

"You were too involved the last time."

Jack laughed, a short abrupt sound without humor. "Involved? I guess you could say that." He sat straighter. "That punk has led a charmed life, but I hope you're planning on putting an end to his good luck."

"That's my plan," Will agreed grimly.

Jack would like nothing better than to see Mick Terrine put away for life and to be the one to lock the door after the man was thrown inside. He'd wanted to do that five years ago, but Terrine had walked away clean from an assault with a deadly weapon and attempted murder. The only witness against him had disappeared, and a high-priced criminal lawyer had proved that Terrine had been "denied his legal right to council" when he'd been questioned after the arrest.

Jack hadn't had to ask why he'd been kept at a distance this time. Emotions had no place in this work. This time there was no detective standing across the table from Terrine, blood splashed on his shirt and pants. No detective with the bad luck of being in the way when Terrine had freaked out just after being arrested and swung with a tire iron, slashing him across the chin and gouging his shoulder.

This time there had been no mistakes. Jack had followed everything from a distance while this murder case was being developed. And if the grand jury indicted the man for first-degree murder, Jack wouldn't be above gloating a little. "I'd like to see him burn," Jack muttered.

"Join the crowd. And he's stupid enough to think he's going to walk without a problem." Will shook his head. "We approached him with a deal for information on the organization, but he's sure that everything will just disappear."

Jack sat forward, resting his elbows on his knees. "It's happened before, Will."

"But I'm going to make very sure it doesn't happen again. Our case is solid."

"You've got a witness, don't you?"

"Sure do. One Alicia Sullivan, a blackjack dealer, consort and confidante of Mick Terrine's. She didn't witness the killing, but she can put him in the hotel at the right time and, get this," Will said, a smile almost curling his lips, "he told her *everything* he did to Prince. Including that bit about the necktie, *and* she's agreed to go in front of the grand jury and tell them everything. We'll get an indictment and a conviction."

"I take it you've got your witness in a very safe place."

"We're keeping her out of sight, no names to the press, and she's listed by number on the disclosure list of witnesses. We don't want to take any chances, just in case Terrine's old man decides he wants to help his kid and protect his own butt."

"One thing you can count on is him trying," Jack murmured. "I just hope he can't get to her."

"We're using 'safe' locations. So far, so good."

"She agreed to spill what she knows?"

"I wouldn't say she actually agreed. She's putting up a good front, but it's obvious she's scared and would turn and run, but we've got the upper hand."

"How?"

"Immunity for her testimony, or jail as an accomplice after the fact. She didn't come to us. We had to go and find her and drag her in. Bottom line is, she's here. She's with Lucy Demera right now. Demera's been with Sullivan since we picked her up. But now I've got a slight problem."

"The reason for this meeting?"

"Yeah. I just found out yesterday that Lucy's walking. She's got a daughter who's expecting a child soon. There are complications and she wants to be with her. She says she has to leave tomorrow at the latest."

At that moment Jack knew where this conversation was heading. He didn't like it. "Just don't tell me you're going to ask me to baby-sit Mick Terrine's mistress for you."

"No, I won't tell you to baby-sit her. I need you to *protect* her for me while we're coming down to the wire, to keep her safe and get her into the grand jury's chambers before ten on Monday morning."

The room was dead silent for a long moment while the two men just looked at each other, then Jack stood and reached for his textbook. "Sorry. You've got my firstborn when it gets here, but I've got to study. If I was a twenty-six-year-old and a full-time student going for the bar, instead of a thirty-five-year-old burned-out cop doing it part time, I'd do it. But my brain has been slowly turning to mush, and I can't lose any time."

"You won't have to," Will said quickly, standing to face Jack across the desk. "You can study all weekend. I just need you to sit in a hotel room with this woman and don't let her leave. You can study all you want to." His frown actually eased a bit as his mouth twitched slightly in what might have been the suggestion of a smile. "She's not hard on the eyes, either, believe me."

Jack smiled ruefully. "I didn't expect Terrine's mistress to be ugly."

Will spread his hands palms up. "Oh, she insists she wasn't his mistress, just his friend."

Jack laughed out loud at that. "Well, everyone has their own definition of 'friend,'" he said, then sobered. "What's important is how valid her testimony is."

"It's pure gold." Will came around the desk and opened the top drawer closest to him to take out a large manila envelope. He opened it and slid a single eight-by-ten colored photo onto the desk, then nudged it across to Jack. "There she is. Alicia Sullivan. The chink in Mick Terrine's armor, the lady he told about the murder of Milt Prince. The woman he joked with about how appropriate it was to have taken him out in the Royal Suite at the hotel."

Jack put down the book and reached for the photo. "Mick Terrine never could keep his mouth shut, could he?"

"Not when he's been drinking and finds himself around a beautiful woman."

Jack looked at the photo in his hand, a candid photo of a woman standing outside a casino on the strip.

"We got that shot when we were tipped she had information," Will said.

"Who called it in?"

"An informant who knew what he was talking about."

Jack studied the photo of a woman tall enough to tower over the doorman at the hotel, and a woman with a striking figure set off by a barely there skirt and a black tank top that hugged provocatively full breasts. A mane of curly red hair fell around slender shoulders, framing a face that was partially hidden by oversize sunglasses, but showed full lips.

A beautiful woman, he thought, but that beauty was outweighed by the fact that she had been with Mick Terrine. He dropped the picture onto the desk, distaste rising in his throat, then he looked at Will. In that moment, Jack knew he didn't really have a choice.

The idea of Mick Terrine walking again because the witness wasn't there was too much for him. And in some way making sure that Mick Terrine was convicted made Jack feel as if he could finally put an end to that part of his career before he left for good.

"All right," he said, and exhaled harshly. "I'll do it."

"I owe you." Will reached for the photo and put it back into the envelope before looking up at Jack. "She's coming here Friday to meet with her lawyer, a public defender. We can make the switch then. Be here at four o'clock, and I'll personally introduce your companion for the weekend, Alicia Sullivan."

Chapter 2

Las Vegas, Friday morning

"You were right. They have the woman."

George Terrine kept his back to his suite on the top floor of the Nirvana Hotel as his assistant spoke. He stared out over the rooftops of Las Vegas into the distance. A windstorm during the night had left a thin veil of dust over the hills that surrounded the city, a muggy brown haze that blurred the horizon where it blended into the clear October sky. It reminded Terrine of how the lines in life got blurred and smudged. And he didn't like that. He liked things to be clear and defined.

Now his son had muddied the waters, blurring and smudging lines that should have been kept clean and precise. Mick had never learned that. And Alicia Sullivan was a perfect example of Mick's carelessness. Mick had seen her, wanted her, and now she was the one person who could bring Mick down and possibly the operation with him.

The police had Alicia Sullivan, just as he'd suspected, but being right only fanned his anger at his son. His hands at his sides clenched into fists as what Mick had said just days ago rang in Terrine's mind. "She's crazy about me, and she's not stupid. She won't sell me out. She knows what's at stake—for all of us."

Stupid and foolish, Terrine thought as he crossed to the built-in bar to the left of the windows. He splashed a healthy serving of bourbon into a glass and tossed off half of it in one gulp. The fiery path it burned down his throat and spread to his middle only underscored the fact it was up to him to clean up Mick's mess, the way he had five years ago. And he'd do it again, one way or another.

Terrine emptied his glass before he turned to Sharp. The totally bald man, tall and thin, dressed all in black, stood silently by the doors, waiting. Sharp had been with Terrine since Mick was a child, and his first name had been lost somewhere in those years. He was just Sharp, and he was also one of the very few people in this world Terrine trusted completely.

"She's talking, isn't she?" he asked, his hand clenching his empty glass.

"Yes, sir. From what I've found out, she's told them that the boy was in Las Vegas and in the hotel around the time of the incident. Mick was drunk. Mick was bragging about offing Prince." His dark eyes never blinked. "And they've got her slated to go in front of the grand jury this Monday."

Terrine knew how weak and foolish his son could be. He'd always thought there was too much of his wife in the boy, that she'd coddled him too much. But that didn't change the fact Mickey *was* his son, hisown flesh and blood, a Terrine. And George wouldn't see his son or the family suffer for taking out some lowlife like Milt Prince, no matter how sloppy Mick had gotten.

"Where do they have her?" he asked.

Sharp shrugged slightly. "Somewhere in the city. I've got a contact who's working on finding the exact location."

Terrine put the glass back on the bar, then looked at Sharp. "Pay whatever you need to pay."

"I am, and I think we'll know everything by tomorrow."

"Good." Terrine crossed the room to come within a couple of feet of Sharp. "You know that it's up to us to save Mick, don't you, Sharp? And if that's not possible, we'll have to work out a contingency plan."

"I understand, sir."

"No matter who gets in the way?"

The bald man stared right at Terrine. "Yes, sir. Just tell me what you want me to do now."

Terrine reached out and flicked the lapel of Sharp's immaculate suit with the tip of one finger. "First, I *don't* want Alicia Sullivan to exist on Monday morning."

The man's dark eyes narrowed, and for a moment Terrine saw a flash of pleasure in the expression. The perfect man for the job. "There'll be no Alicia Sullivan on Monday morning," Sharp said.

* * *

Las Vegas—Friday afternoon

Jack and Will walked silently along the corridor of the second floor of the courthouse, heading toward the back stairs that went down to the rear security entrance. As they came to the flight of stairs, Jack stopped by the rail and looked below. There was no one in sight on the lower level. He glanced at his watch, then at Will, who had stopped beside him. "I thought you said they'd be here at four?"

Will shrugged. "You know how client-attorney meetings go. They'll be out soon. Meanwhile, we've taken all your things to the new location."

Jack frowned. "New location?"

"We've been at the old place long enough."

Jack could feel himself tighten. "Why?"

Will inhaled as his hand gripped the rail. "It looks as if she's tried to contact someone on the outside. When we picked her up, she said there was no one. She had no family, no friends she wanted to call. But she made a call from the hotel room early yesterday morning, about half an hour after midnight."

"To who?"

"That's just it. We don't know. It was a collect call, and there's some sort of snafu. They're having a hell of a time figuring out where the call went. We're doing what we can to get the number as quickly as possible."

"What did she say about the call?"

"We haven't brought it up with her. No reason to give her any idea we know until we have a clue about what we're dealing with."

"And that's why you're moving her?"

"Partly, and partly because it's time."

Jack glanced down at the empty corridor on the lower level. *Move and keep moving* was the theory behind keeping someone safe. Sitting still for two days was about the longest Jack would care to do. "Who knows where she'll be?"

"Me, Chief McDermot and a handful of plain-clothes who helped clear the area and secure it."

"Who?"

"Clearwater, Paven, Nicholes, Ramerez and Stewart."

All men Jack knew or had heard of.

"And Thomas Storm. He's my liaison and problem solver."

Jack trusted Storm completely. He inhaled and felt the pressure of his police special pressing into the small of his back where he'd tucked it into the waistband of his jeans. Any time a Terrine was involved, Jack knew that a gun was a paltry weapon to carry. He touched the scar on his chin. A cannon wouldn't be much better, he thought, then caught movement below.

He looked from the rail and saw a plainclothesman come into view from under the balcony overhang—Paven. The dark-skinned man was dressed in what Jack would have charitably called yuppie clothes—a pink polo shirt, beige linen slacks and loafers. Paven looked up and down the corridor, then motioned behind him, and two women hurried into view. Another cop followed in the rear—Stewart. In a plain white shirt and dark slacks, the thin blond man looked more like a cop.

Jack recognized one of the women as Lucy Demera, middle-aged and dressed in civilian clothes that
did little to flatter her stocky figure. Then he saw the
second woman, and no one had to tell him she was
Alicia Sullivan.

Her hair was brilliant, a riot of wildly teased curls,
and a true red. It fell partway down her back and
around her shoulders. A pale yellow T-shirt accentu-
ated high full breasts, and close-fitting jeans showed
off slender legs that looked as if they went on forever.
She stopped as Paven came up behind her, and when
he spoke to her, she turned. Jack saw her face without the protection of the sunglasses she'd worn in the
photo.

He wasn't shocked by the fact she was truly beautiful, that large eyes shadowed by lush lashes and a full
mouth touched by a bronzed lipstick dominated a
delicately boned, heart-shaped face. Or that her skin
was almost translucent and touched with a pale glow
of a tan, or that her neck was graceful, her nose small
and straight. What shocked him was the fact that he
was seeing a woman who would make any man look
twice, yet she didn't touch him except to make a de-
gree of anger and disgust rise in him at the thought of
a man like Mick Terrine having her.

Paven disappeared from view. Then Alicia Sullivan
turned to Lucy Demera, spoke quickly, and whatever
she said, Lucy shook her head immediately. The Sullivan woman moved closer, speaking quickly as she
pressed her hand to her stomach and grimaced.

Lucy reached out to take the woman by the arm,
motioning for her to stay right where she was, but the
woman kept talking to her. Lucy said something to

Stewart at the same time Will touched Jack on the shoulder. "Come on. They're waiting for us. Let's go down there and you can meet your weekend company."

Jack didn't move. He suddenly wasn't anxious to go down there. A part of him didn't want to be close to this woman at all. He stared at her, seeing her take another step toward Lucy, then he realized the matron wasn't her main objective. She moved past Lucy and toward the rest-room door, but before she could take more than a few steps, Lucy had her by the arm, stopping her dead in her tracks.

"Let's see what's going on," Will said as he hurried past Jack and moved toward the stairs.

Jack followed Will, his sneakers making no sound on the hard marble flooring, then started down the stairs in the wake of the other man. But before they got to the bottom, Lucy and the Sullivan woman were nowhere in sight, and the cops were standing with their backs to the closed rest-room door.

Paven saw Will and moved toward him. "They're in there. The woman said she's going to be sick."

Jack could see the rush of relief in Will. "As long as she lives until Terrine's put away," he muttered.

The rest-room door opened and Lucy came out into the corridor. She looked a bit flushed, but her expression cleared when she saw Will standing there.

"I'm glad you're here," she said as she swiped at her graying hair.

"What's this all about?" Will asked.

"She knew we were meeting you down here, but the minute we got near the rest room, she told me she was going to throw up. I figured it's better in there than in the car, so I checked the rest room, and it's clear. Last I heard, she's inside throwing up."

"Is she really sick?" Will asked.

"I think she's got a bad case of nerves, and who wouldn't if they knew they were going to testify against the likes of a Terrine?" She looked at Jack. "Jack, I didn't believe it when this guy told me you'd agreed to do this. I thought you and the Terrines were a thing of the past."

"So did I until Will talked me into this." He tucked his fingertips into the pockets of his jeans. "I agreed to sit in a hotel room and study. A byproduct of keeping the witness safe and out of sight."

"I wish you well." She turned and pushed open the rest-room door to call out, "Hurry up in there."

"I'll be out in two minutes," Alicia Sullivan answered in a muffled voice.

Lucy looked at Will. "Do you want me to go in after her?"

"No, let her be sick in peace."

"All right, whatever you say, but I'm out of here."

"Good luck with the new baby," he told her.

"Thanks," she said, then hurried away.

Jack watched Lucy leave, then looked up and down the corridor. The hairs prickled at the back of his neck. He didn't like being exposed like this, standing out here like some lackey waiting for the woman. *Move and keep moving. Only stop when you're safe.* He knew those rules well. He glanced at Will, who looked at his watch, then up at Jack.

"Give her two more minutes," Will said.

Jack nodded. "If she's not out here by then, *I'll* go in after her."

* * *

Ali had thought she could never be a criminal the night she'd been arrested with Brad, but now she knew she'd been right. Since she'd walked into the court-house, her heart hadn't stopped pounding, and fear had tightened a knot in her stomach. Now, even though she was right where she said she'd be at four o'clock, she couldn't breathe properly or get rid of the terrible feeling that this switch would never work.

Sitting on top of the tank of the toilet in the last cu-bicle in the rest room, she rested her feet on the closed lid and listened to every noise outside. She'd never been the twin with an imagination, the one who went on flights of fancy, on trips of daydreaming. She'd been grounded, secure and happy to finally have sta-bility.

Now she was here in the pink-and-white marble rest room, fully expecting the police to crash through the door and find her sitting on the back of the toilet waiting to impersonate her sister.

"Get a grip," she muttered, hugging herself and pressing her fingers into her upper arms. She knew why she was doing this—for Lydia, and partially for Alicia. Maybe a bit for herself. And that focused her thoughts. Besides, no one had even looked at her twice when she'd come into the building or when she stepped into the rest room ten minutes ago. In jeans, an over-size white sweatshirt and tennis shoes, with her hair tucked under a baseball cap, she'd blended in with the other people in the corridors and slipped in here with-out incident.

Now all she had to do was wait until Alicia got here. All she had to do was spend a weekend in a hotel room so Alicia could go to Lydia. That was it. She wouldn't talk to anyone she didn't have to, and she'd get out of here on Monday and back to sanity.

She jumped when she heard muffled voices out in the corridor, then the door clicked open. With her heart in her mouth, she stared at the door of her cubicle, wishing she'd locked it, and listened to footsteps strike the hard marble floor. "I'll check it out," she heard a woman say, then a door being thrown open to bounce back against the metal walls of a cubicle. She felt the vibration in the wall of her cubicle under her hand, which was pressed to cold metal to steady herself.

Another door hit a cubicle wall, then another, the jarring vibration coursing up Ali's arm. Just when Ali knew the next door would be hers and she'd be exposed, she heard Alicia. "Get out of my way!" her sister gasped.

Then the door to her cubicle crashed open, and Alicia was there in a blur of wild curls. She slammed the door behind her, threw the bolt into place, then with a flashing smile for Ali, started to cough and make horrible choking noises. A rap on the door made Ali jump, and the woman she'd heard before called out, "What's going on?"

"I...I'm sick," Alicia mumbled, the smile never faltering. "Please, leave me alone for a few minutes."

"All right. Just make it fast."

As footsteps headed off, Alicia leaned back against the locked door, crossed her arms over her chest and made a horrible gagging sound that made Ali's stomach churn. "Thanks," she choked, but never looked away from Ali. Footsteps struck the marble floor, leaving, then the door swished shut, and silence filled the room.

Alicia, with wild hair, mascara emphasizing long lashes, color high in her cheeks and that smile as if she were the cat who'd eaten the canary, gave a thumbs-up. Ali scrambled off the back of the toilet and, without saying a word, reached out to her sister. For a long moment they just clung to each other, then Ali stood back, tears pricking her eyes. She'd missed her sister more than she'd even known.

"Thank God you made it," Alicia whispered, the smile faltering now. "How's Lydia?"

"The same. I didn't tell her you were coming—in case it didn't work out."

"But it did—so far. Now we have to hurry." She dropped a huge shoulder bag onto the floor by her feet, then began to unzip her jeans. "We don't have much time."

Ali put her purse on the back of the toilet and undressed as quickly as she could. In just a few seconds, Ali was in Alicia's clothes, clothes that, she was thankful, weren't quite as tight on Ali as they had been on her sister.

Alicia zipped up the jeans, pulled the sweatshirt over her head, then tugged the cotton fleece down over her hips and stood back. She stared at Ali, who was tugging at the yellow T-shirt, then without a word, she reached out and pulled the clip out of Ali's hair.

"We have to loosen you up a bit," she said in a whisper.

She hunkered down to fish around in her purse, then stood with a brush in one hand and quickly teased Ali's hair until it was in wild disarray. Dropping the brush back into her bag, she got out her makeup kit and told Ali to stand still. In just a couple of minutes she stood back and looked at Ali, then turned and cautiously opened the cubicle door until it rested against the wall.

Without moving, Ali could see the two of them in the mirrors that filled the opposite wall above the sinks. "Not bad," Alicia said in a low voice as she twisted her hair and pushed it under the baseball cap.

With Alicia beside her, Ali saw the double reflection, two people, one of them Alicia, one of them Alison. And even Ali had to admit that outwardly she was Alicia. She was the sister who was a free spirit, who never took anything seriously and who lived for the moment. The one who'd been so deprived of stability that she never gave anyone a chance to build it around her.

Then she looked at Alicia, who had scrubbed most of her makeup off. Yes, Alicia was Ali, the sister who loved stability, sameness, safety. The sister Alicia had always called "boring but cute."

"Do you have everything I need?" Alicia asked.

Ali looked away from the reflection, reached for her purse and gave it to her sister. "Here. Take this. The plane tickets are in there, along with some cash and my ID."

Alicia didn't look inside. She just slipped the strap over her shoulder, then reached down for her huge bag and gave it to Ali. "And here're all my worldly goods."

Ali had no doubt her sister wasn't exaggerating by much. No ties, nothing to pull her down. Carry everything in a bag so she could take off when the spirit moved her. She settled the heavy bag on her shoulder, its weight almost as much as the pressure from worry she felt on her chest.

"Don't frown like that," Alicia said. "No one's going to know the difference. The new bodyguard never met me, and the old one's out of here as soon as her replacement shows up."

The door to the rest room opened without warning, and Alicia climbed up on the closed toilet seat as a woman called out, "Hurry up in there."

"I'll be out in two minutes," Alicia called back in a weak voice.

The door shut, and Alicia hopped down and faced Ali. "She's all right, just nervous about her daughter's baby. Her name's Lucy Demera. She said she would be handing me over to a new bodyguard today before we went back to the hotel. Just keep to yourself, stay put, and I'll be back here Monday morning at eight-thirty. Tell them you need to use the rest room before you go in before the grand jury."

She reached into her own purse that Ali was carrying and pulled out a wad of tissues. "Use these. Hold them up to your face until you feel safe."

Ali took the tissues, then Alicia pulled her to her. The hug was so tight, it took her breath away. "I'll make it up to you, sis," she whispered in her ear, then let her go and scrambled up onto the back of the toilet.

This is crazy, Ali thought, but she couldn't back out now. When Ali gave her a thumbs-up again and silently mouthed, "Go," Ali took a shaky breath and walked out of the cubicle. As the door thumped behind her, she closed her eyes, braced herself, then headed for the exit.

With the tissues pressed to her mouth, she pushed the door open and stepped out. The air in the corridor seemed close and stuffy, and that feeling wasn't helped by the fact that Ali almost walked into four men directly in front of the door. Two men stood back, one in what looked like resort clothes, the other in a plain white shirt and dark slacks. The other two were closer, a worried-looking bear of a man in a gray suit, and another man.

He stood nearest to her, not more than three feet away, and the air grew even more oppressive. His features weren't anything remarkable, maybe a bit harsh, with plains and angles. His sandy-blond hair, which was swept back carelessly from his face, was a bit shaggy and long enough to lie on the nape of his neck.

But the minute her gaze met the clear blue of his eyes, she felt a jolt go through her. She looked away, thankful for the protection of the tissues at her face. Her eyes dropped to a strong mouth with a full bottom lip, then to his jaw and scar—a faded line that cut jaggedly across his clean-shaven chin—which gave an edge to his looks. If she reached out and touched it, she knew it would feel irregular, but without roughness, beyond the vague suggestion of a shadowy beard.

Catching herself, she instinctively took a partial step back, letting her gaze drop, skimming over the man's navy sweatshirt, well-worn jeans, and scuffed running shoes. She felt embarrassed to have been staring at the man, yet when she glanced back up at him, he was staring right back at her. His blue eyes studied her without any apology, direct and cutting in their assessment, as if he'd never seen her before.

Why hadn't Alicia told her about this man, about all of them? And where was the matron?

"Are you all right, Miss Sullivan?" the man in the gray suit asked. "You look a bit pale."

She glanced at him and saw a tag fastened to his front jacket pocket—Detective William Stanton. At least he wasn't looking at her as if she were an alien. "I'll be all right," she mumbled into the tissues as she looked around. There wasn't a matron anywhere.

The man with the blue eyes, seeming to read her mind, said, "Mrs. Demera's gone."

Ali looked back at him. "But she's supposed to be my bodyguard."

"She *was*." He inclined his head toward her. "Will told you about the change. I'm your new bodyguard. My name's Jackson Graham. But you can call me Jack, and now it's my job to make sure you get to court on Monday morning in one piece."

This was all wrong. Ali could deal with pretending to be Alicia if a woman was with her over the weekend, but instinctively she knew that being with this man, this closely, for so long, could make it impossible. She was having trouble just thinking straight when he looked at her, and she couldn't imagine a whole weekend of his closeness while she pretended to be someone she wasn't.

"But I'm supposed to have a matron. It's . . . it's a rule that a woman guards a woman," she stammered, not knowing exactly what she was talking about, but thinking it sounded logical.

"We promised you protective custody," Detective Stanton inserted quickly. "And, believe me, you've got the best with Jack protecting you."

"I'll leave you completely alone as long as you abide by the rules," Jack said as he reached out and took her by her arm. He started to lead the way toward the back of the building. "Right now we've wasted enough time. We can't stand here any longer."

She knew how true that was. Alicia couldn't get out of the rest room and head for the airport until they were gone. But the moment Jack touched her arm, Ali felt as if he had snatched away what little control she still had. She hated the sensation, and letting a man like this control her was even more unsettling. Before she thought, she jerked away from his touch and stopped, her hand dropping from her face as she turned to look at him.

"Take your hands off me," she muttered, feeling foolish for overreacting and wondering if she'd just blown everything.

But when she looked at the others, at their tolerant expressions, she knew she was acting exactly the way Alicia would. Alicia didn't do anything she didn't want to do. Lifting her chin in the same way Alicia had ever since she could remember, she looked up at Jack and forced herself to make direct eye contact. "You might be taking care of me, and I'm not at all sure that's right, legally, a male cop watching a woman and all, but if you have to do it, don't you touch me again. Do you understand?"

He stared at her, then unnerved her by leaning toward her, coming so close that she seemed surrounded by the scent of mellow after-shave mingled with maleness and the heat of his breath brushing her skin. "Understand this," he said in a deep tight voice, "that as long as I'm your bodyguard, you do what I tell you to do without asking questions—no matter what it is. If I touch you, it's because I have to, not because I want to.

"Right now we're leaving this place. Stay to my left and slightly behind me and keep pace with me. Do *you* understand that?"

All she understood right then was if she didn't get some buffer of space between herself and this man, she wouldn't be able to do anything. She knew she was blushing, and her first instinct was to turn away, to build much-needed distance. But she couldn't, not as long as she was supposed to be Alicia. Her sister never backed down. So she forced herself to keep eye contact. "I'm not stupid."

"Now, why would anyone think you're stupid just because you've been playing house with Mick Terrine?" he drawled, his sarcasm so thick she could have cut it with a knife.

She flinched inside, and her face felt like fire. "You . . . you can't talk to me like that," she said, her voice annoyingly unsteady. She looked at the man in the gray suit. "This isn't legal, is it?"

The man shrugged. "Short of cruel and unusual punishment, Jack can do whatever he wants to over the weekend to make sure you're in one piece on Monday. Right now I've got to go." He placed a hand on Jack's shoulder. "Good luck, and I'll be in touch," he murmured.

Jack didn't once take his eyes off Alicia Sullivan. Seeing her from a distance was a totally different experience than being this close to her. First, every time he inhaled, he caught a strange mixture of scents. There was a hot scent of perfume, which he'd expected, yet under it he could detect a delicate scent of wildflowers. And her eyes, a stunning shade of deep green shadowed by lush dark lashes, were wide and touched with a vulnerability that he never expected to see in a woman like this.

From a distance, he'd felt impervious to her, but now he was having second thoughts. She was blushing, really blushing. Her face had flooded with high color, which only emphasized the delicate bone structure. And he had an overwhelming urge to ask her what right she had to blush, to look almost embarrassed when she'd been with a man like Mick Terrine.

Then Will was talking, telling him he was leaving, but Jack didn't look away from the woman in front of him. He nodded to Will, said goodbye, then spoke to the woman. "Stay to my left, back half a pace, and move. We're leaving. Now."

This time she didn't say a thing. Instead, she hiked the ridiculously oversize purse higher on her shoulder, fell into step to his left and went with him to the back doors. Paven led the way, Stewart walked behind them, then Paven opened the doors. Jack paused before stepping out into the shimmering heat, saw three cars idling within ten feet of the doors and recognized the men driving the front and rear cars. Clearwater and Ramerez, the detectives Will had told him were on the case.

He scanned the parking area beyond, but couldn't see any movement on the ground or on the roofs that overlooked the area. Will had secured the area well.

"We're going to the middle car," he said. He glanced at her, meeting the direct intensity in her green eyes. "Get in on the passenger side and slip down low in the seat."

"Anything else?" she asked.

"Move fast and don't stop," Jack said, then he started out the door.

Chapter 3

J ack didn't have to tell Ali to move fast. Sudden uneasiness was making her even more nervous. At first she'd thought the bodyguard and all the security measures were overkill, put in place to keep Alicia from running off and disappearing. But now she was beginning to think that something else was going on here.

She hurried after Jack out into the oppressive heat of the late afternoon, staying close to him on the way to the car, but not close enough to make physical contact. The passenger door was ajar and she tugged it open wide, then scrambled inside. She was grateful that the engine had been idling and so the interior was filled with refreshing coolness.

Out of habit, she reached for the seat belt as Jack got in behind the wheel, but almost jumped out of her skin when he reached out and grabbed her purse strap.

With one sharp tug, he jerked Ali sideways and partly down onto the seat by him. "What . . . ?" she gasped, trying to keep from going sideways into his lap.

"I told you to get down low when you got in!" he ground out as he let go of the purse strap.

"I was just going to fasten my seat belt," she mumbled, sliding toward her door more, staying low, as she pushed her purse onto the floor by her seat. She refused to rub her shoulder where the purse strap had bitten through the T-shirt into her skin.

"A car accident is the least of your worries," Jack muttered as he put the car into gear and started to drive.

His words only deepened her uneasiness. She could barely see above the dash, but she saw the car that had been parked ahead of them leading the way out of the parking lot. The other car was probably behind them. Bodyguards. Why were they going to all this trouble just for a witness? Had Alicia tried to run away before? She doubted it. That would have been Alicia's first reaction to confinement.

She looked at Jack, not missing the tension in the hands that gripped the steering wheel. He must be expecting the worst. And he'd be right. Alicia wouldn't make this easy on anyone.

From her vantage point low in the seat, as they drove toward the Strip, all Ali could see were the tops of buildings with garish signs and the sun glinting off glass walls that soared into the desert sky, now touched by the colors of twilight. Without looking at Jack, she said, "Isn't this a bit much?"

"What?" he asked.

She turned to him. "The bodyguards and all this cloak-and-dagger stuff?"

"What do you think we should do? Rent a limo, take you to the Sands and put you up in the penthouse suite?" he asked, casting her a slanting glance tinged with derision. "Or maybe we could just send out engraved notices to let Terrine know where you are?"

That jarred her. "Terrine? He's in jail, isn't he?"

"Junior is. But his father's not, and neither is his father's organization."

She stared at him. "You mean it's like the mob?"

"Give the lady a prize."

"No, I mean, no one believes that stuff about the mob, do they?"

He glanced at her again. "What do you think a father who has no morals and every gun in the city at his disposal *and* knows there's one person who can put his son in jail for life, or worse, is going to do to that person? Is he going to send her a thank-you note and flowers, or maybe throw a party in her honor?"

Oh, God, this wasn't because of the trouble Alicia had caused and Ali knew right then just how much trouble her sister had drawn her into. Her stomach churned and sickness burned the back of her throat. "You think that his . . . his father would try to . . . ?"

"To have you killed?" Jack looked right at her as they stopped for a red light. His eyes narrowed, and for a moment she was certain he could see into her soul and worse yet, hated what he saw. Then he shrugged and turned his gaze back to the road as he said bluntly, "I think that George Terrine would have you removed from the face of the earth without blinking an eye and regret it about as much as he would swatting a fly."

"Removed?" Ali echoed, unable to look away from Jack. "What do you . . . ?"

"Killed. Rubbed out. Eliminated. Dead," Jack said, his gaze riveting. "You act as if you've never thought about it."

Heaven help her, she hadn't. She'd worried about fooling people, about deceiving people, about whether Alicia could get in to see Lydia without anyone knowing there had been a switch and whether Alicia could get back here without anyone being the wiser. Even if Alicia had given the police problems. But she'd never dreamed that someone would want her sister dead to keep her from talking. And God help her, for the next three days, everyone would think *she* was her sister.

Ali closed her eyes to block out the world while she tried to make sense out of what was happening. Alicia had always been a free spirit, acting before she thought, jumping in with her eyes closed, seldom weighing the cost. But there had never been anything like this before. Ali felt tension in her body, her neck going into a spasm because of the uncomfortable position, but when she tried to shift to ease the tightness, Jack's hand on her shoulder stopped her.

"Stay down," he said, applying pressure to keep her in place.

She sank back, her head at an angle against the seat, and looked at Jack. "You're serious, aren't you?" she managed, knowing the answer before the question was completed.

"Does this all seem like a joke to you?"

"No, it doesn't," she admitted. It seemed like a nightmare that was gaining speed with each passing moment. Alicia hadn't mentioned anything about anyone trying to kill her. She'd talked about the Terrines using Ali and Lydia to put pressure on her. But that was mild compared to the idea of someone being willing to kill Alicia to keep another person safe.

Jack darted her a sharp look, then flexed his hands on the wheel. "This is as good a time as any to get something straight with you."

"What?"

"I have no use for Mick Terrine, or any of the Terrines or their friends."

And that included Alicia. "I understand," she murmured.

"No, I don't think you do." He fingered his jaw, skimming over the pale scar there, then let his hand return to the wheel. "But that doesn't matter. Just understand that my opinion of Mick Terrine is that he's a slime, a low-life jerk, and as long as he gets what's due him, that's all that counts."

"And for him to get what he's due, I have to testify."

"You've got it, kid."

"And if I don't testify?"

He slowed the car even though they were in the middle of a block and looked at her. "What?"

"If I don't testify, what would happen?"

"Damn it, you made a deal."

"A deal?"

"What's wrong with you?" he demanded. "Don't you understand anything?"

Heat flooded her face again, but she tried to stay calm. "Humor me," she said tightly. "Explain this deal to me one more time."

"Okay. I'll try to make this simple and use single-syllable words you can understand. You talk, you get off."

"And the Terrines would be after me for the rest of my life."

"That's your choice. Will offered you the Witness Protection Program through the federal marshall's office. He said you declined."

Alicia was more of a fool than Ali had thought, but it figured. Alicia wouldn't want to be confined, not even if it meant protection from the Terrines. "But if I don't testify?" she prodded.

"Terrine might or might not get indicted and held over for trial, and you'll be charged with accessory to murder after the fact." ·

While his words sank in, Jack drove the car onto a side street and up an incline into a parking lot. Ali barely saw the glass-and-steel structure of a hotel that towered at least forty stories into the desert sky before the car went down a sloping ramp and came to a stop in an alcove formed by cement block walls on either side. Ali faced the fact that until now, she'd thought the most important thing in this world was making sure that Lydia got to see Alicia, that it would help her foster mother get through the surgery.

Until now.

As the car stopped, Jack touched Ali on the shoulder. She looked at him, meeting eyes that glinted like pure steel. "Are you going to keep your part of the bargain?" he asked.

She touched her tongue to her cold lips. What could she tell him? That Alicia usually ran rather than face anything head-on? That Alicia thought leaving was the most logical way to deal with adversity? Her heart sank.

For a moment she let the possibility that Alicia might not come back form, then she pushed it away. One thing she knew about her twin was that she loved Lydia, and she had genuinely wanted to see her.

But if she didn't come back on Monday?

A ruddy-faced man wearing a panama hat came up to the passenger side of the car, but Jack didn't make a move to get out. His hand now lay heavily on her shoulder, and his eyes never left her face. "Well, where does letting a murderer get off fit into your idea of morality?"

The man opened the door on Ali's side, but she didn't move, either. She didn't want to take a chance on having Jack jerk her back. "Can I sit up?" she managed.

He stared at her, then drew back from her and said, "Get up, and when I give you the word, get out and head toward those doors." He pointed to an entry to the bottom of the ramp that was marked Service. "Don't look up. Move quickly. Don't wait for me and get inside."

As Ali straightened and grabbed her purse, the heat from the outside began to invade the interior of the car through the open door. She saw a man disappear through the doors Jack had pointed out, and another man was checking behind dumpsters set against the cement block walls. After what seemed forever, the man who had gone inside stepped back out and waved toward the car.

Then Jack moved abruptly. "Now!" he said, and Ali scrambled out into the blanketing heat. The man in the panama was behind her, and she could see his hand resting inside his jacket. Heart pounding, she almost ran toward the doors, keeping her eyes on the cracked concrete under her feet. She didn't take a full breath until she was through the open doors and in the cool dimness.

Then someone had her by her upper arm, and she didn't have to turn to know it was Jack practically dragging her along the dull green corridor. His hand almost circled her arm, firm enough to keep control, yet loose enough to cause no discomfort physically. Emotionally was another matter. The contact was overwhelming to Ali, disturbing in its confinement, yet reassuring in its support. She didn't look at Jack.

She stared straight ahead down the cavernous hallway, at the painted walls marked and chipped by delivery carts and boxes. As she forced cool air into her tight lungs, she saw someone holding open the doors of the first elevator. Then she was in the elevator car with Jack and two of the other men.

As the doors slid shut, Jack released her, but stayed close enough so she could feel the heat from his body through her thin clothes. She shifted just a fraction of an inch to get some distance from the sensation, and determinedly stared at the floor numbers as they flashed on and off over the door.

"Miss Sullivan, these men are detectives, Ramerez and Clearwater. They'll be around all weekend."

Alicia glanced at the two men, guessing that the swarthy man with the pencil-thin mustache and deep brown eyes was Ramerez, and the man in the hat was Clearwater. She nodded to them, received nods in exchange, then there was just silence.

On the ride upward in the elevator her mind couldn't let go of what Jack had said. The Terrines would kill Alicia to keep her from testifying, and for the next three days, she was Alicia.

The elevator stopped at the thirtieth floor, and after everything Jack had told her earlier, she braced herself as the doors slid open. She didn't know what she expected to find there, but she was relieved when she saw the dark-skinned man who had been with her in the corridor at the courthouse. He had a side holster, something she hadn't noticed before, and his hand rested on his gun.

She also noticed his visible relief when he saw the occupants of the elevator, then he moved quickly to his left.

"This way," he said. "It's clear."

The next thing Ali knew she was being whisked out into the hallway, thick carpet under her feet and pale blue fabric walls all around. In a blur she was taken down the hallway to a door being held open by the other man from the courthouse. When Jack, Ali and the dark-skinned man were inside, the door was shut with a resounding click.

Ali stood just inside the door. The sitting room in front of her was decorated in a style she could only call elegantly flamboyant. Two couches covered in a rich paisley fabric faced each other across a low square cherry coffee table. A Queen Anne desk stood against the right wall, an elaborate entertainment center and bar on the opposite wall. The open doors on the right and left showed two bedrooms done as extravagantly as the sitting area. Heavy silk draperies covered the far wall, shutting out all outside light.

She glanced at the suitcases sitting to one side of the entrance, a stack of thick books piled on the floor beside them. Jack and the other man were moving around the suite, looking and checking, then came back to where Ali was standing. "It's clear," Jack said to Ali, then he glanced at the other man. "Paven, tell Will I'm settled in for the duration."

"Yes, sir," Paven said. "If you need anything, I'm next door with Ramerez. Clearwater and Stewart are on the other side. This part of the floor is cleared of guests. Just ring. And if there's an emergency, we'll hear anything that happens."

Jack crossed to where the books were stacked, picked up the top one, then looked back at the man. "Seems as if Will thought of everything."

"He tried. He wanted you to be happy being here." Paven looked embarrassed. "I mean, he—"

"I understand." Jack tossed the book back onto the pile with a cracking echo that made Ali jump, then he looked at her. "Is there anything you need?"

I need to get out of the nightmare, she wanted to say but didn't. She just shook her head. She watched Jack walk the man to the door and talk to him for a moment. When the man was gone, Jack closed the door, threw the security bolt and came back to where Ali still stood. He reached out a hand. For a moment, she thought he was going to touch her again, and she braced herself for the contact, much the same way she'd braced herself when the elevator doors had opened. But he didn't touch her. Instead, he reached past her and bent to pick up the large, worn leather suitcase.

His blue eyes met hers. "Let's get settled in. It's going to be a long weekend." He glanced around the room. "Take your pick of the bedrooms."

The idea of being in a room where she could close the door and shut out this madness was eminently appealing. To be able to think without this man distracting her was even more appealing. The closest room would do just fine. She picked up the remaining suitcase, a new-looking blue one she assumed was Alicia's, and turned toward the open door of the bedroom. "This will do fine," she murmured.

"Alicia?"

Her sister's name stopped her, and she turned back to Jack. She knew she didn't want him calling her by that name. "I answer to Ali," she said.

His eyes narrowed. "You can smoke in your room with the door closed. Not out here. Is that understood?"

Ali hoped all his rules would be this easy to keep. She'd never smoked, unlike Alicia who had started smoking when she was sixteen, believing it made her look more mature. "All right," Ali agreed.

"That's rule number two for the weekend."

"What's rule number one?"

"You aren't to set foot outside of this suite until Monday morning—not for any reason. Understood?"

She didn't even want to come out of the bedroom. "Of course," she said. "Any more rules?"

"The old ones are still in force, and the rest we'll make up as we go along."

"Fine," she said, then turned and went into her room.

Ali had heard about Las Vegas hotels, about the tacky glitz in their decorating, but there was none of that here. This room was as fashionably elegant as the sitting room. It was large, at least twenty by thirty, and dominated by a four-poster bed and a huge bank of windows covered by beige silk curtains. The soft roses, greens and turquoises were easy on the eyes and a welcome change after the harsh colors that had bombarded Ali ever since she'd arrived at the airport.

She dropped the suitcase onto the thick carpeting, reached to close the door, and as the barrier slowly swung closed, she had a last glimpse of Jack standing where she'd left him. He was staring at her, not moving, his face stamped with a tight expression of distaste.

As the door clicked shut, Ali felt all the air go out of her. She crossed to the bed, dropped down on the edge of the soft rose velvet spread and found herself facing a bank of mirrors mounted on the side wall.

But she didn't see herself. She was looking at Alicia. Alicia wearing makeup that Ali seldom wore, with hair that was untamed and bright, in clothes that were vastly different from the tailored slacks, straight skirts or walking shorts she usually favored.

She stood and crossed to the suitcase. Opening it on the floor, she dropped to her knees and sorted through the contents. She pushed aside the short skirts, low-neck blouses and short shorts until she found a pair of old jeans, a plain white tank top and, under some heels and backless sandals, a pair of old running shoes. She quickly stripped, dressed in the new clothes, then found a silver clip in the cosmetic case and pulled her hair back off her face.

When she looked in the mirror again, she could almost see herself there—except for the makeup. As she started across to the adjoining bathroom, there was a knock on her door, and she veered over to answer it.

Jack stood in the entry and for a moment he stared at her as if her appearance shocked him, but he didn't comment on it. Instead, he asked, "Are you hungry?"

It shocked her to realize she was starved. She had barely eaten since Alicia's phone call. And amazingly, despite the situation she'd been caught up in, she could feel her stomach rumbling. "Yes, I sure am."

"I'll put in a call for food. What do you want?"

"Anything's fine with me," she said.

That brought a real frown to Jack's face, and she knew her mistake. Jack had obviously been briefed on the woman he was guarding, and that meant he knew Alicia was really picky about food. She didn't eat any meat at all, preferred her vegetables raw or steamed, and she drank only bottled water or white wine. That limited what Ali could order.

"Actually," she said quickly, "I think a salad would be fine."

"Water or white wine?" he asked, verifying what she suspected about his briefing.

The idea of a bit of alcohol appealed to her right then. Maybe it would help settle her nerves. "White wine, please."

Jack looked at the woman in front of him and wondered when he'd ever gotten such conflicting signals from another person. He knew her background. He'd read the file Will had given him, that Alicia Sullivan was the sort of woman who breezed through life, who didn't have any roots, any family or any attachments beyond the moment. Yet that didn't stop him from sensing something in the woman in front of him that didn't ring true.

If he wasn't sure she was the woman who'd been involved with Mick Terrine, he would almost think she was embarrassed by the connection. And now, in her old clothes, her hair pulled back from her face, she looked . . . He searched for the right word, and all he could come up with was "vulnerable." And that shook him.

He blocked out the image of her wide green eyes, the way her hand worried the knob of the door and the way she nibbled on her bottom lip, almost stripping it of the remnants of pink lipstick. "Is there anything else you need? Cigarettes?"

She shook her head. "No, just food, thanks."

Jack found himself staring at the way wispy curls of hair caressed her skin, and he determinedly turned his back on the sight. He crossed to the phone in the sitting room and dialed Paven's room. He told him he needed food and got the response, "No problem. What do you want?"

He ordered quickly, then asked, "How long will it be?"

"Maybe an hour. Stewart and Ramerez are taking a break, so we can't move until they're here for cover. But we'll get it to you as soon as we can."

"No problem," Jack said.

"We'll call first," Paven said, then hung up.

Jack put the phone back and stared down at the black plastic instrument. He sensed Ali standing near him. For some reason he hesitated turning to face her, but when he finally did, he wasn't prepared for his reactions. She was close to him, not more than a few feet separated them, and she was holding one of his law books. The book looked huge and heavy in her delicate grasp, and she was frowning at Jack, which drew a fine line between her remarkable eyes.

"I thought you were a policeman," she said.

"I am. I have been for thirteen years."

She glanced down at his law book, then back at him. "Are these yours?"

"All mine." He didn't reach for the book. "I graduated from law school, and now I'm studying for the state bar exam." He finally took the book from her, a bit shocked to feel the heat from her hands still on the cover material where she'd gripped it. He glanced at the book, then back to her. "That's why I need to have peace and quiet this weekend. I have to study."

She pushed her hands behind her back and studied him from under her dark lashes. "Isn't that a cliché, the burned-out cop who eventually ends up being a lawyer?"

Maybe he was burned out, but he didn't feel like a cliché. "*This* cop is going to be a prosecutor."

"You don't like being a cop?"

That took him aback. He'd never thought in terms of liking or disliking his work, just moving on to something that wasn't life and death every day. "It's all right. But I want to do other things." He moved away from her, out of the range of that delicate perfume that seemed to cling to her. Another contradiction in the woman. "The food will be here in an hour or so."

As he put the book on the desk, he wondered if this woman was predictable at all. Then he found out she was just what Will had said she was when she finally spoke. "An hour? But I'm starved. I can't wait a whole hour."

As he turned, the woman he saw across from him fit more and more into the mold he'd expected from Alicia Sullivan. She stood with her hands on her hips, her chin lifted, and he squared to face her, actually bracing himself. "Sorry, it's going to take an hour. They're in the middle of two of the men taking a break, and they'll be back then."

She moved toward him. "How many men does it take to bring up some food?"

"One man," he said, "but it takes a great deal more to cover that man and to cover us while he's busy with the food."

"Can't you go and get the food? I'll stay here like a good girl."

"I'm not about to even go running down the hall to get peanuts out of a machine for you. Rule number one. *We* don't leave this suite."

The small chin lifted a bit higher. "I'm starving. I thought you were supposed to be taking care of me."

"I'm sure men have been willing to take care of you since puberty, but get this straight. I'm a bodyguard, not your flunky."

Even though color rose in her cheeks, she rolled her eyes upward and exhaled in a rush. "All right, all right. You don't have to get personal. You made your point, but how about something as simple as room service? Surely you can handle some bellhop who brings the food. I've never seen one who looked like he could take out a fly."

This was what he expected, and in some way it was a relief. No more delicate woman who looked vulnerable and out of her league. This was the Alicia Sullivan he could deal with, and he let his anger grow. "I can handle anything except some spoiled woman who got involved with a man like Mick Terrine."

The color in her face deepened, and she looked down at the floor. "Forget it," she mumbled.

Her ability to blush was unnerving, and he tried to grab at his anger. Going toward her, he got within two feet and stopped himself before he reached out to touch her chin, to make her look at him. "Let's get one more thing straight, Miss Sullivan."

"What else?" she muttered, not looking up.

He stared at her bent head, almost thankful he wasn't looking into those green eyes right now. "I don't want to be here. I'm only here as a favor to Will. The bottom line is we can do this the easy way. We can get through the weekend and get you to put Mick Terrine where he belongs, or—" he paused until she finally looked up at him "—we can do it the hard way."

Ali could barely force eye contact with Jack, and she wasn't about to ask what the "hard way" was. "I don't want to be here, either," she said with real truth. "But I am. And I'll get through it. Now, is that all, or is there anything else you want to *get straight?*"

The sarcasm that crept into her voice surprised her. For a split second she'd sounded just like Alicia. An Alicia who could face anyone and never give in. Stubborn and so sure she could hold her own with anyone. Alicia had always had a way with men, just as

Jack insinuated. She'd been able to get them to do what she wanted one way or another for as long as Ali could remember. But judging from the set of Jack's jaw and the way his blue eyes riveted her to the spot, Alicia might have met her match in this man.

"Just follow the rules," he muttered tightly, and as he turned from her, he tossed over his shoulder, "and keep your door closed if you're going to smoke."

She watched him move toward the other law books stacked by the door, pick one up, then without looking at her again, go to the couch and drop the book on the coffee table with a resounding crack. The sound made Ali jump, and she turned from the sight of him and went back into her room.

It was becoming shadowed with evening since the heavy draperies covered the windows and no lights were on. Ali hated the dark, but the idea of bright light didn't appeal either. She didn't want to have to look at anything too closely, not any more than she wanted to stand here by the closed door listening to every sound that Jack made in the next room. She didn't want to hear him moving around, a door open, then close, a shuffling and the sound of scraping as if furniture was being moved.

She moved quickly over to the television set in the entertainment unit on the wall opposite the bed, snapped it on, and as the flickering blue-gray light from the screen filtered into the room, she slipped off her shoes and climbed onto the bed on top of the spread. She reached for the remote control on the nightstand and was going to flip the channel, but stopped when she heard the name Terrine.

Chapter 4

On the television an attractive blond newscaster was reading the news, a box inset on a blue background in the upper left-hand side of the screen, holding the words, "Held without Bail." It took Ali a moment to realize the woman was talking about Michael George Terrine, Jr., the only son of Michael George Terrine, of Las Vegas.

She sat very still, watching the screen as clips were shown of a tall gray-haired man identified as George Terrine; then the clips changed to a man being escorted by uniformed police from a courtroom. Across the bottom of the screen it said, "Mick Terrine, alleged murderer."

Mick Terrine looked to be in his late twenties, with dark hair slicked back from a long face with shadowed eyes, a heavy jaw, a smug expression touching a full-lipped mouth. She watched him wave aside a reporter who got too close, then stop and deliberately glare into the television camera.

Ali stared at him, uneasiness sliding up her spine. The newscaster's voice was lost on her, and all she was aware of was the eyes of Mick Terrine. Then his image was gone, replaced by a tall, slender, dark-haired man who stood in front of a weather map. "Now, the weather for Las Vegas and the state..."

Ali slowly lay back on the bed. What had possessed Alicia to be with Mick Terrine? A man who had killed another person, who had friends and family who, according to Jack, would do anything they had to for him? They wanted to stop Alicia from testifying in front of the grand jury, to save the son of George Terrine from his fate.

Ali closed her eyes, turned onto her side and drew her knees up to her stomach. What had Alicia said? She didn't want to let anyone know she had family, that they could put pressure on them? Hadn't Alicia had the slightest idea that the Terrines could do a great deal more than put pressure on her?

She heard a noise above the drone of the television, then realized that Jack was singing. In a slightly off-key bass, he was singing the old Rolling Stone song "Satisfaction." And despite his lack of musical talent, the sound of his voice was a comfort to her. He was right outside her door, and something in Ali believed that, despite Jack's feelings about Terrine or Alicia, he'd do his job and protect her.

Gradually she began to relax, and as Jack started back on the first verse of "Satisfaction," she felt herself drifting off. She floated in softness, rolling and tumbling like a feather on an errant summer breeze.

Free, light, without worry or concern. She relished it and let herself go. For a few moments, she was outside all this pressure.

Then from somewhere she heard a voice, deep and smooth, saying, "Mick Terrine, the only son of a man who has been a force in Las Vegas for over twenty years . . . Mick Terrine . . . Mick Terrine . . ." The name rang like a chant through her being, then she saw him coming toward her out of a swirling haze.

Dark and intense, his eyes burned into hers as he came closer and closer. "You're dead," she heard him say, the words echoing through her even though his lips weren't moving. He cocked his finger as if it were a gun and made a popping sound. "Bang, you're dead, Alicia, dead."

She wanted to scream that she wasn't Alicia, but nothing would come out of her tight throat. She wanted to run, but she couldn't move. The darkness was all around her, terrifying darkness, yet Terrine could see her, and he kept coming toward her.

"Dead, dead, dead," he chanted, and then he was in front of her, so close she could almost feel him against her. That's when she realized there was a real gun in his hand, the barrel pointed right at her breast.

In slow motion she could see his finger tightening on the trigger, pulling it back. When she heard the click and saw fire shoot out of the barrel, her world exploded and a scream tore from her throat.

It echoed all around her, ripping her out of the dream and back into consciousness. She opened her eyes to a blinding brightness. Someone grabbed her by the arm, and all the fear she'd had in the dream came rushing along with her into consciousness. The world was a blur of light and movement, and Ali instinctively struck out with her free hand, her knuckles striking something hard and cold. Then she was being jerked upward off the bed.

For a moment she felt like a rag doll, dangling in the air by one arm, then as voices yelled, "What in the hell's going on? What's wrong?" she was being drawn into heat and strength.

"No, no," she gasped, balling her hands into fists and pushing against the ungiving strength of her captor.

"Calm down, calm down." The words were a deep rumble in her ears and a tingling vibration against her forehead, her breasts and her stomach. "She had a nightmare," someone said.

Then she stopped, knowing with certainty that this wasn't Mick Terrine who'd captured her against him. She was out of the dream, and she was inhaling a mixture of heat and maleness that was the essence of Jackson Graham. She froze, her forehead pressed against his chest, her eyes closed so tightly colors exploded behind her lids.

The dream, the threat from Mick Terrine, the terror. She took an unsteady breath, and for an instant she felt the heavy thumping of his heart against her breasts along with the distinct sensation of being threatened—but not in a physical way.

"Let me go," she gasped, disturbed by the knowledge that she found herself wishing this man would hold her forever and protect her from the entire world. What a stupid idea! She couldn't hold on to Jack, no more than she could control Alicia. She pushed away to escape, so she could think clearly, and the contact was broken.

She fell awkwardly back onto the bed, the overhead lights flooding the room. She focused on snug jeans molded to hard thighs, then the snub-nosed revolver Jack held by his side in his right hand. Movement behind Jack drew her attention, and she saw Paven and Ramerez, both with guns, both looking harassed and intense. She could hear others moving around in the outer room.

"I'm sorry," she mumbled, pushing with unsteady hands at her mane of curls that had been released from the clip while she'd slept.

Jack dropped to his haunches in front of her, tossed the gun onto the bed, then reached out and took both her hands in his. There was a moment of being surrounded by heat, strength and gentleness, then Ali looked down at his hands on hers. She watched him gently skim over the back of the knuckles on her left hand, barely touching a huge welt that she knew was going to darken into a stunning bruise.

"No real damage," he murmured. "But we were damned lucky the gun didn't go off when you hit it."

She stared at his fingers on her skin, strong and square-nailed and soothing. And for a moment she felt mesmerized, then realized that Jack was talking to her and she had no idea what he was saying. She drew her hands away from his, and he let her go. Pulling both her hands to her stomach, she looked at Jack, who was straightening to his full height over her.

His hair was mussed and vaguely spiked in front as if he'd been raking his fingers through it. In the bright light, the scar on his chin seemed paler and more ragged. Deep shadows cast from the overhead lights hid the expression in his eyes.

"I'm sorry, what did you say?" she said.

"I asked if you wanted a doctor to look at that."

Her hand was beginning to throb, and she covered her sore hand with the other and shook her head. "No, I'm all right. I was just . . . It was a nightmare."

"Mick Terrine is great nightmare material," he said, then spoke over his shoulder to the other two men without looking away from Ali. "It's all clear. Go on back."

"Are you sure?" Paven asked.

"Yeah, everything's fine," Jack said, and he didn't speak again until the two had left. Ali heard the outer door open and close, then Jack said, "I was on my way in to tell you the food was here when I heard you scream."

The scream. She could still feel it deep inside her. And the reason for it hadn't left her mind. As if the thought of the man conjured him up, she was suddenly aware of the television and a newscaster saying the name Terrine again.

She didn't want to look, but much the same way a person is drawn to look at a horrible accident, she found her eyes drawn to the screen beyond Jack. The same picture of Mick Terrine she'd seen earlier, which apparently had prompted the nightmare, stared back at her. And the nightmare was closer and closer to the surface.

Jack looked down at Ali, her hair loose, her face almost free of makeup and deathly pale. The first time he had glimpsed her at the courthouse, he'd been surprised that a woman this pretty couldn't touch him.

But since she'd walked out of the rest room, that had all changed. He'd felt shocked that she was actually vulnerable and that she'd chosen to be with Terrine. And when he'd heard her scream, he'd never known such fear. His heart rate was still a few beats above normal.

He just wanted to protect her from everything. He rubbed his hands together as if that would erase the feel of her from his memory. There was no way he wanted to be overwhelmed by a need to keep her safe for any reason other than that she was a means to an end in the prosecution of Mick Terrine.

He looked away from her to see what she was staring at on the large television, and just the sight of Mick Terrine brought everything into focus. As he turned back to Ali, he felt an anger that he understood completely, an anger that gave him a reprieve from all the emotions he'd felt in the past few minutes.

"Admiring him?" he asked, and knew the stupidity of the question when he saw the raw fear etched on her face and reflected in her eyes. She held up her bruised hand, as if it was enough to ward off his words. Then, with a shake of her head that sent her curls tumbling around her shoulders, she turned and scrambled across the bed, getting to her feet on the far side.

Without another look at Jack, Ali escaped into the sitting area, into softer light, background music drifting in through speakers positioned around the room, and the smell of food filling the air. A large silver tray with domed covers, along with a glass of wine and a steaming cup of coffee, had been put on the low square table that separated the two couches.

Ali crossed to the nearest couch and sat down on the edge of one of the cushions. And she didn't turn as she sensed Jack coming closer. When he slipped around the table to sit on the couch facing her, she didn't take her eyes off the tray. She watched his hands remove the covers from the food, one revealing a plate holding a large steak, baked potato, vegetables and crusty bread, the other a large glass bowl containing a salad with every type of green and topped with shredded carrots.

Jack motioned to two small bottles by the bowl. "Oil and vinegar." Then he reached for his plate and moved it closer to his side of the table.

Ali stared at his meal, felt her stomach rumble, then made herself reach for the salad and begin to eat it. As she speared a lettuce leaf, she glanced at Jack, cutting his steak. Rare, just the way she liked it. She dropped her fork by the bowl and reached for the wine. Sipping the cool liquid, she closed her eyes for a moment, but opened them immediately when the image of Mick Terrine came back to taunt her. She gulped almost half the wine, before she put the glass back on the table.

"Something wrong with the food?" Jack asked.

"No, not really." Not anything forgetting about Mick Terrine wouldn't cure, she thought.

"Did the news on Mick Terrine ruin your appetite?"

The man could read minds. "I guess so."

"Is it that hard for you to think of being the one to make sure he's put away for good?"

That brought her head up, and she saw Jack sitting forward on the couch, the coffee mug cradled in both hands. "What?"

"Was Mick so good that you hate to think it's over between you two?"

"You don't understand," she murmured.

He sipped some steaming coffee, his eyes over the mug never leaving Ali's face. "What's to understand? Some women like men like that." He put down the mug and sank back against the cushions. "You must have thought he was pretty damned special at one time. Maybe you still do."

She felt her face flame. "What I think of the man is none of your business."

"Was it the pretty-boy good looks, or the money, or the power? Some say that power is the strongest aphrodisiac there is."

Even as her face burned, she found herself wondering the same thing. Why would Alicia look twice at Mick Terrine? "What difference does it make?" she muttered.

"None, probably," he said with a vague shrug of his shoulders. "But I've heard that a woman needs reasons for getting into bed with a man. What's the old joke? A woman says, 'Why?' and a man says, 'Where?' Why would a woman want to climb into Mick Terrine's bed?"

Ali had never wanted to get into any man's bed, and she couldn't begin to fathom what would make Alicia want to be with Terrine. She knew about deprived childhoods, about lack of love, about lack of nurturing, but that wasn't a reason to get close to a man as destructive as Terrine apparently was. And it bothered her. She didn't know what to say to Jack, what he could understand, or what she could, either. But before she came up with a coherent answer, Jack lifted one hand and held it palm out to her.

"I forgot," he said, "that you and Mick were just friends, acquaintances. Isn't that what you told Will?"

One thing she knew for sure about her sister—Alicia wasn't a liar. If anything, she was bluntly honest. If she told them she hadn't slept with Terrine, she probably hadn't. "It's the truth," she managed.

His mouth lifted in a poor imitation of a smile. "Sure, whatever you say. And Santa Claus is real, I suppose."

A qualifier came. What did she really know about her sister now? Alicia was seldom at home, and her life had been her own for years. But she couldn't let Jack keep talking like this. "Who are you to judge what anyone does?"

His face tightened and his words came out low and intense. "I know Terrine. I know what a slimy bastard he is. I've seen what he's done to women and to other men. You might not know it yet, but you're damned lucky that SOB's locked up."

"Sure, and I get to be target practice for his people."

Jack sat forward, his food forgotten. "You get to do the right thing, then get out of here. And Terrine gets what he's deserved for years."

"You hate him, don't you?"

"No, hate's too soft a word."

Now she sat forward. "Why?"

He hesitated, then echoed her own words back to her. "What difference does it make?"

"You're passing judgment on me. I'd like to understand why you, as a professional law-enforcement officer, let yourself get emotionally involved in the fate of the man."

He picked up his napkin and dropped it over his half-eaten dinner as if the remaining food offended him. "Did you ever think of becoming an attorney? You know how to ask cutting questions."

"I'm just curious," she admitted truthfully.

"I'll make this simple. Five years ago, I arrested Junior and he didn't take to it. In fact, he used a tire iron and left his mark." He tapped his chin. "I didn't get this to impress anyone."

"He did that with a tire iron?" No wonder he didn't like the man.

"Just think what he could have done with an ax," Jack said, but there wasn't a trace of humor in his face.

"That's why you hate him?"

"Partly, and partly because he walked. He didn't have his 'rights' protected. He got off and left me holding the bag. Damn straight I hate him. I hate what he stands for and I hate what he does to people. And maybe, just maybe if you do what you should, he'll have to pay. Maybe this time his father won't be able to get him out of it."

"His father—?"

"A witness disappeared, and a slick lawyer got the charges dropped by proving that Junior didn't have legitimate counsel during his questioning."

"The witness disappeared?"

"We never found him." He glanced at her salad. "I thought you were starving."

"I was," she murmured, visions of people floating facedown in the river flashing through her mind.

"Do you want something else?"

Concrete boots. That's what they always threatened in the movies. She shivered involuntarily and shook her head at Jack. What she wanted was to get out of here, but the only place to go was the bedroom, and she didn't want to be in there and dream again. She glanced at the wall clock. Seven-thirty. Lydia and Alicia should be together by now. All she had to do was stay here and pretend.

She picked up her wineglass and stood. "Was the witness really important?"

"So important that most of the case disappeared with him."

As she paced the room, she saw the open textbooks on the floor by the coffee table. She finished the last of the wine, then twirled the goblet between her hands and continued to pace. She turned and asked, "Is there any more wine?"

"They only sent up the one glass. I thought that's all you allowed yourself."

She shrugged. "I guess so."

His plate had been pushed to one side, and a book was open in front of him. "If you need to smoke, go in the bedroom," he said without looking at her.

"No, thanks," she said, still twirling the goblet.

He glanced up at her and frowned. "You're a bundle of nerves. Go and have a smoke. I used to be a smoker, and I remember how I craved it when there was pressure or tension. I still crave it. That's why I don't want you smoking in here."

"How did you quit?"

"I was in the hospital and couldn't smoke for three weeks. When I got out, it seemed stupid to start doing something I'd wanted to quit for years. But I don't proselytize. Do what you want—just don't do it in here."

She couldn't begin to keep up a charade of smoking for the weekend, and she didn't want to be in the bedroom letting a cigarette burn in the ashtray for effect. "I'm quitting," she said. "I think it's time."

He raised an eyebrow. "Just like that?"

"Just like that. I don't need three weeks."

"Well, I'm impressed. I never would have guessed you had such strength of character."

The implied idea was anyone who messed with a Terrine was hardly well endowed in the character-strength area, and she found his sarcasm cutting. She put the goblet on the table, then crossed to the draped windows to put distance between herself and Jack. What she craved right now was fresh air and the feeling of space.

She reached out, touched a button on the wall, and the heavy fabric slowly began to part. As the world outside was exposed, the lights of the Strip flooded into the room, bathing every color in a spectrum of brilliant flashing colors.

Las Vegas was spread at her feet. But before she could do more than take in the ribbons of lights far below, the flashing signs of casinos and hotels, and the desert sky of black velvet touched by the glow of the city, she heard Jack yell.

"Hey, don't do that!" She turned and saw him standing, his books scattering to the floor.

"What—"

Her words were cut off by a low explosive sound and a burst of energy whizzing past her. A mirror on the far side of the room shattered, and Jack screamed, "Down! Get down! Now!"

Then he was coming at her, literally leaping over the low table and, the next instant, tackling her. He jerked her down to the floor and covered her body with his. For a heartbeat she was lost in heat and silence and a sense of security that she'd never known before. Then Jack drew back just enough to look down at her.

His face was pale. She could feel the tension trembling in his arms, and his heart hammering against her breasts. "Are you all right?"

"I think so," she gasped. "What happened?"

Before he could answer, the door to the suite burst open, and Paven and Clearwater were there, guns drawn. Jack didn't even look at them. He never took his eyes off Ali. "Across the way," he said. "One shot."

Shot? Someone had shot into the room. No, someone had shot at *her*. She closed her eyes, her ability to breathe greatly diminished, and that sense of security she'd felt for an instant gone completely.

"Draw the curtains," Jack said, "and get Will on the line."

Ali opened her eyes and Jack filled her senses. He was over her, his face no more than inches above hers, his rapid breathing fanning her cold skin. She saw the way his jaw worked, the veins throbbing in his temple, and she could feel the tension in him where his body pressed against hers.

"Someone . . . shot at us?"

He looked down at her, his eyes riveting her. "Us? *You,* Miss Sullivan. Someone shot at *you.*"

"Clear," Paven called, then Jack rolled to one side and Ali was free.

The curtains were back in place, hiding what damage the shot had done to the window, and Clearwater was on the phone while Paven walked through the suite from room to room. Ali twisted onto her side, then pushed herself into a sitting position on the floor.

She looked up and saw Jack get to his feet in one fluid movement, then look down at her. "What in the hell were you thinking of?" he demanded tightly.

She got awkwardly to her feet, hating his towering over her, and brushed at her clothes. "I just wanted to see outside," she mumbled.

"And to hell with the rules?"

She looked up at Jack. His paleness was almost gone, but the tension still there in every line of his face. "Rules?"

"Never open the curtains. Never stand in front of a window. And *never* do it at night with the lights on behind you!"

She cringed at the rising volume of his voice and tried to brace herself the way she knew Alicia would do. But she couldn't. She hadn't known not to open the curtains or stand at the window. No one had told her the rules, and she'd almost been shot.

"I'm sorry," she managed. "I didn't..."

Jack took a step toward her and for a moment she thought he was going to grab her and shake her. Instead, he rocked forward on the balls of his feet, coming to within inches of her face. "Get your things, Miss Sullivan. We're out of here."

"What?"

"Move, and don't ask questions."

His expression told her it wouldn't do any good to ask anything, and it might just make him shake her the way she had thought he was going to before. Quickly she went around him and hurried into her room. She stuffed the clothes into the suitcase, and when she came back into the sitting-room with her bag in hand, Jack was by the couch talking on the phone.

Jack listened to Will, knowing what the man would say even before the words were out. "Move and keep going. Check in with me when you stop, but don't tell me where you are. Just make sure that woman's in court on Monday. Meanwhile, I've got a lot of checking to do in this department."

"Damn straight," Jack muttered and caught movement out of the corner of his eye. He glanced at Ali as she came into the room, suitcase in hand, and that surging need to protect her flooded over him. Damn it, all she had to do was look at him with those huge green eyes and he felt as if he would gladly go and slay a dragon for her.

That thought almost made him laugh out loud. There were no dragons and he sure wasn't any knight. He was just caught in a rotten situation. Will was speaking, and for the life of him, Jack had no idea what he was saying. "Sorry, what's that?"

"I said Storm will have your cash and papers for you. Keep it clean and neat. I'll pick up on this end."

"I'll call when I can." Jack hung up and spoke to Ramerez by the door. "Is everything in place?"

"Ready when you are," the man said.

He looked back to Ali, wishing he saw a glimpse of the contained, almost hard-edged woman he'd expected. "Have you got everything?" he asked her.

She had the huge purse over one shoulder and her suitcase in her other hand. "I think so. What are we doing?"

With her hair loose and brilliant, there was no way she could leave without being noticed. This woman couldn't be anywhere and not turn heads. "We're leaving, and you're going to have to do exactly as I say without question. Agreed?"

She didn't speak, just nodded.

Paven came back into the room and crossed to Jack. "Here you go." He handed Jack two pairs of dull green coveralls, along with two billed caps. "The service elevator can be kept clear for about ten minutes, and a linen-service truck is parked at the side entrance. Get in the back. Clearwater will drive you to an unmarked car. Storm will meet you and brief you."

"Good. Clear the hall and signal when it's set." Paven nodded, then crossed and took Ali's purse and suitcase, stopping to pick up Jack's and put it under his arm. "What about your books?" he asked.

Jack glanced at the heavy texts and knew his hopes of studying this weekend were shot to hell. "Make sure they get back to my place."

"Sure thing," Paven said, then left.

As the door clicked shut behind him, Jack moved toward Ali and held out the smaller of the two coveralls. "Put this on over your clothes."

As she did so, he put on his own coverall and tugged on the cap. He turned again to Ali and his worst fears came true. Even the drab clothing didn't disguise her, the rough cotton not hiding the curve of her hips, the high breasts or the slender waist where she'd cinched a fabric belt. Sexy even in baggy olive drab, he thought ruefully.

As Ali tucked her hair under the cap, she had a vivid flashback of doing the same actions before she'd gone into the courthouse earlier in the day. When the last strand was hidden, she looked at Jack, who had put on the coveralls. He pulled the cap low on his forehead, then returned her gaze, his eyes narrowed and skimming over her from head to foot.

For a second she felt exposed and had the distinct impulse to fasten the last button of the outfit, and as his eyes met hers, she knew how wrong she'd been. There was disgust so strong in his eyes it made her cringe.

"Lose that belt." The order was clipped and quick.

"What are you—"

Before she could finish the question, Jack came closer and quickly manipulated the buckle to undo it. He pulled the belt free of the side loops, tossed it to one side. Then he tugged at the green material to loosen it at her waist.

"Why did you—"

His eyes drilled into hers, her question cut off as sharply as if he had put his hand over her mouth. "This isn't a Las Vegas review," he muttered. "Maybe Mick Terrine likes the cheap look, but it won't work if you're going to pass as a delivery person." The fire in her face intensified. "Slouch a bit, keep your eyes down, move quickly and, for heaven's sake, try to act inconspicuous."

Damn it, she hated the way he could unnerve her with that cold voice and impersonal look. Yet he seemed able to do it at the drop of a hat. "Any other orders?" she asked tightly.

He moved back from her, but his gaze never faltered. "You heard what Paven told me?"

She nodded.

"All right. We're leaving as soon as he signals us. No matter what happens when we step out of this room, don't stop. Someone will be with you at all times. Just keep going and get the hell out of here."

Suddenly the idea of leaving the confines of the suite took on a scary note. Up till now escaping this place had been an appealing idea. Now she was running for her life.

Chapter 5

Three sharp knocks on the door were followed by someone calling, "Now!"

Jack started for the door. "Here we go," he murmured as Ali came up behind him. He opened the door and then they were out in the hall. "Slowly," he said, and she had to force herself not to run the sixty feet to where a man she hadn't seen before held the elevator doors open. The journey to the man dressed in a Hawaiian shirt and jeans seemed to take an eternity. Just when she felt as if she'd be sick from the tension, she reached the elevator.

She stepped into the car, Jack followed, then the Hawaiian-shirted man came in behind them as the doors slid shut. Jack looked at the man, who was a match for Jack in height but probably carried an extra twenty pounds around his middle. "This is Detective Nicholes," Jack said to Ali.

Nicholes inclined his head toward Ali, his pale eyes shadowed and neutral, then turned to stare at the door, his hand resting on a bulge under the side of his shirt.

Ali stood between the two men, not touching, and as the car slid silently downward, she tried to control the hammering of her heart by taking in short shallow breaths.

"It helps if you breathe in through your nose and out through your mouth—slowly," Jack said.

She glanced at him, but he was staring at the floor numbers flashing above the doors. "Pardon me?"

"In through the nose, out through the mouth. They teach you that first thing when you're in training at the academy. Fear isn't all bad, and even if you're scared spitless, it helps you focus."

"Does it really work?"

He slanted her a look, and for a moment she could have sworn that his expression softened, that the tension at his mouth eased. "Yes, it does," he said, then turned away.

Ali only had a chance to do it twice before Jack said, "Just two more floors, then we're out of here."

Ali saw the light flash the number one. Then the elevator stopped and the doors opened. The thin blond man was there, looking very unassuming—except for the gun held in his hand, which was pointed at the elevator.

The gun lowered slowly when he saw the occupants, then he motioned to their left. "That way."

Jack quickly took Ali by the upper arm and hurried her out of the elevator and down what looked like the same corridor they had gone through coming in.

Nicholes kept pace behind them, and they bypassed the doors they'd come in earlier and went along a corridor that sloped downward and ended at a set of huge metal doors. Nicholes moved ahead of them, slid one of the doors back with a noisy protest of squeaks and grinding, and Ali saw the white metal body of a huge truck backed into a space lined by cement block walls.

The sound of its rumbling engine bounced off the walls, and the odor of exhaust fumes was everywhere. Then they were out into the blanketing heat and the yellow glow of night security lights. Two metal stairs at the back of the truck had been slipped into place, the back door rolled up, and Ali was rushed up the stairs and into the trailer. The whole time, she felt Jack's hand at her back. She stepped into a space where huge laundry carts and stacks of brown-wrapped packages lined the sides.

Before she could turn to look at Jack, the door was rolled down and most of the light was gone. "Stay calm," she told herself as she groped to her left, and grabbed the metal handle of a cart. As the truck started off, she steadied herself, and tried to see through the shadows. As her eyes adjusted, Jack was no more than a dark blur about three feet from her.

"Take off those coveralls and the hat," he said, his voice sounding muffled.

Silently she did as he said. "What do I—"

"Just drop them. Someone else will take care of them."

She tossed the clothing in the general direction of one of the carts, then shook out her hair. "Are you going to tell me where we're going?'' she asked as she raked her fingers through her curls.

"I don't know where we're going."

"I thought you planned this."

He came closer. "I didn't plan on doing anything but sitting in the hotel and reading all weekend." His voice, tight and low, came to her through the darkness. "It's your boyfriend's family or friends who changed the plans. Now we're going to move and keep moving until it's safe to stop."

Ali hated the darkness, and with the lack of light she became uncomfortably aware of everything else about Jack. His size, the aura of maleness that clung to him, the heat of his body in the confines of the truck and the fact that he kept rocking toward her as he talked.

"We'll basically just keep you alive until Monday morning." He rocked closer. "Then we'll head back for the court."

His words jolted her, then the truck lurched and Ali stumbled sideways, reaching out and colliding with Jack. His chest was against her, his hands at her shoulders, and both he and Ali slid backward until a stack of parcels at her back stopped the fall. Her hands were pinned between her breasts and Jack's chest, and she felt the heavy beating of his heart under her palms.

She swallowed hard, but didn't move. It wasn't as if this hadn't happened before, his body against hers, the distance between them diminished to nothing. And it wasn't as though she hadn't been totally aware of him the first time. But now there were no sounds of shattering glass or whizzing bullets to distract her, or men shouting and movement all around. There was just soft darkness, the muffled roar of the engine, the vibration of the truck as it traveled through the streets of Las Vegas—and Jack.

Then he spoke, so close his breath fanned her face with heat. And she shivered slightly. "Sorry."

Nothing had prepared her for her reaction to this man, a man she hardly knew, a man who disliked the woman he thought she was. Yet she couldn't move; she couldn't even speak. And when he moved back, she couldn't for the life of her figure out why she felt a moment of deep disappointment and a sense of abandonment.

Abandonment? That made no sense at all, yet she knew the feeling well. Over the years, after every foster-home change, the feeling of abandonment had been her constant companion. Finally it had gone and hadn't reared its head again until this very moment. It didn't make sense, not any more than the fact she wished with all her heart she could tell him the truth.

She felt the air stir as he moved back farther, then the truck began to slow. "Get ready," Jack said, his voice disembodied in the darkness. "When the door opens, just follow me."

The truck stopped completely, then the door began to roll up, and Ali could see Jack for a moment. He was turned from her, heading for the door, then he was outside. She moved quickly after him, aware of a night sky filled with a brushing of twinkling stars, but none of the glare and glitter she'd expected.

She hesitated at the exit and saw single-storied homes on large lots. So, they were in a residential neighborhood. She'd never thought there was anything like this in Las Vegas. The city had always meant casinos, hotels and restaurants to her, not middle-class tracts.

The metal steps were gone, but before she could jump down, Jack was there reaching up, his hands spanning her waist. For a split second, she was suspended in air, then gliding down, brushing Jack's chest with her hips then her waist and her breasts. She literally held her breath until she felt the pavement under her feet. He let her go, the space between them grew, and although Ali knew there were other men there, they were only shadows, mere suggestions of people. Yet Jack was remarkably clear in front of her.

Ali wondered if being surrounded by danger did this to everyone. This becoming totally focused, seeing things with a clarity that was almost painful, experiencing things that they had never even known existed before? She felt light-headed and confused.

"Over there," Jack said, pointing to a black Jeep parked by the curb in front of a house. The Jeep's engine was idling and the doors were open, so the inside light was a dull glow in the night.

A tall rangy man in dark clothes came out of the shadows and nodded to Jack. "Let's go."

Without responding, Jack took Ali by the arm, his fingers light but compelling, and hurried her to the Jeep. Nicholes moved away from the Jeep to allow Ali and Jack access to the passenger door. When Ali would have gotten in the front, Jack said, "In the back."

Wordlessly, she squeezed in behind the front bucket seat and onto the small bench seat behind. Then the man who had met them got in the passenger side and slammed the door while Jack jogged around to climb in behind the wheel.

She'd thought just the two of them would be heading out, but she felt a sense of real relief that a second man was coming with them. Jack shut the door, jammed the Jeep into gear, then drove off. They wound through streets that could have been any middle-class neighborhood in any town in the country. Ranch-style houses, huge trees, two cars in every driveway. Then they turned onto a street lined with small businesses.

All the time he drove, Jack kept checking the mirrors, staying just below the speed limit, and finally they were putting the city behind them. Lights became few and far between.

When Jack turned onto what looked like a two-lane highway, the man in the passenger seat spoke. "Surprised you're in on this, Jackson." His voice was low and rough.

"Me, too," Jack muttered, and glanced to the side, his face illuminated by the lights of an oncoming car. "Are you going to tell me what happened back there?"

"The best-laid plans..." The man had been checking the mirror on his side off and on since they'd started out, and now he turned to look out the back window. Ali felt as if she were invisible, as if he were looking right through her, but at last he made eye contact. "I'm Thomas Storm, homicide detective. So, you're the Terrine witness."

She gripped the edge of the seat so tightly her hands tingled. "Yes, I—"

Jack cut her off. "Alicia Sullivan, alive and kicking. No thanks to Will or your people. Now, what did they find out about that fiasco?"

Storm glanced into the side mirror again as he spoke. "The shot came from the hotel directly across the street. Same floor, same position. They've shut off the room and called in forensics, but it's empty, and I doubt they'll find anything."

"Who talked?"

"Good question."

Jack glanced at Storm. "You'd damn well better have an answer soon. There's a hole in this operation that the *Queen Mary* could sail through, and I don't feel like laying down my life when I'm within inches of getting out of this business in one piece."

"I never thought you'd really leave," the man countered.

"Well, just watch me walk away after this mess is done."

Ali was beginning to feel invisible again, and she leaned forward. "Where are we going?"

"Away from here," Jack muttered.

"We can't just run like this," she said.

"What do *you* suggest we do?"

"Go to another hotel, or maybe to the jail." The idea of being safe behind locked doors appealed to her now. "It'd be better than being out in the open like this."

Jack glanced in the rearview mirror, and for an instant he made eye contact with Ali. She felt the impact of his glance. "Someone in the department is feeding information to Terrine's people. So we have to move and stay out of sight, or your lover won't have a witness against him on Monday."

Lover? The word made her feel sick. A man who would have her sister killed certainly didn't qualify as a lover for anyone. "We just keep driving?"

Storm cut in. "You two do." He motioned to the side of the highway. "Let me out."

Ali felt her chest tighten. She'd thought—no, she'd hoped—that Storm would be in this for the duration, that he'd be a buffer between Jack and her. It was going to be just the two of them again. She looked around at open land with no lights in sight. The only illumination came from the Jeep's headlights and the moon, starting its rise in the dark sky.

Jack drove onto the shoulder of the road, and Storm got out, then ducked to look back inside. "Everything you need is in the glove compartment." He glanced at Ali, then to Jack. "Good luck to both of you."

"Yeah, we'll need it," Jack said. Then Storm closed the door and began to walk back the way they'd come.

As Jack drove onto the road again, Ali looked over her shoulder and saw Storm heading into the night. In a heartbeat, he was swallowed up in the shadows and lost from sight.

"Get up front if you want," Jack said.

Ali didn't have to be asked twice. She scrambled around the floor console to the front, then sank into the bucket seat and snapped on the seat belt. The Jeep sped up, driving off into the unknown, and Ali knew that all there was between herself and the terror of the Terrines was this man beside her.

* * *

Sharp walked into the darkened office on the floor below the penthouse suite and braced himself. He knew George Terrine hated failure. He hated the weakness in his son, that part of Mick that couldn't measure up. Part of him hated his son. Yet that didn't change the fact that Mick was his only son—a Terrine. And Mick must be protected at all cost, at least for now.

Sharp didn't say anything as he closed the door and stepped into the shadows. The man knew he was there. He knew everything.

Through the darkness he saw movement and caught the scent of an expensive cigar hovering in cool air. The high-backed swivel chair behind the desk moved slowly back and forth. It faced windows that overlooked the Strip, but the draperies were tightly closed to shut out the view. Smoke from the cigar curled toward the ceiling above the chair back.

Sharp went closer.

"What happened?" Terrine asked, his voice disembodied in the darkness.

"It looked like a good setup, but it didn't pan out."

The chair swiveled, and Sharp heard a hissing intake of air. The end of the cigar glowed enough to expose Terrine's face. His eyes drilled into Sharp through the haze of smoke trickling out of his mouth. The silence stretched unbearably. Another man would be babbling by now, trying to make an excuse that Terrine would buy. Not Sharp. He just waited.

Finally Terrine exhaled and said, "Is she lost to us?"

"No, sir. She's on the chart. Our man made sure of it."

Terrine fell silent again, and the chair started to move again, back and forth, slowly. "They'll tighten up on her security even more and drop off the face of the earth."

"They can't."

"Are you sure?"

"Yes, sir. You have my word on it."

Terrine stood, moving through the shadows to come around the desk and approach Sharp. He came so close that the bald man felt the smoke from the cigar sting his eyes. But he didn't retreat. He kept still and kept silent.

"You do it personally," Terrine said. "Clean up this mess."

Sharp seldom did direct work for Terrine—relegation was his style—but this gave him a familiar rush, the rush that came from being the hunter. "Yes, sir."

"My world has been full of fools lately. Don't you fail me."

"You have my word on it. She's dead."

The night seemed vast and empty to Ali. As the Jeep sped along the highway, rushing past flat dark land, isolation bore down on her, and her only line of safety was the man silently driving.

Ever since she'd climbed into the front, Jack hadn't spoken at all. And Ali had had more than enough time to think, to assimilate and have fear settle like a heavy weight behind her breastbone.

She nibbled on her lip, the lipstick long gone, and she held tightly to the sides of the bucket seat. She saw the glow of lights up ahead, but before she could do more than see a few buildings clustered on either side of the highway, the Jeep was past and heading on into the unending night.

She looked at Jack, but could barely make out his profile in the low light from the dash. "Are we going to drive all night?" she asked.

He didn't say anything at first, and for a moment she thought she had been completely shut out of his world. The sense of isolation she'd experienced in the truck earlier came back, growing at an alarming rate, along with the sense of being out of control. Old feelings she'd had in the succession of foster homes. No place to hold on to, no place to put down anchor. She hadn't felt that way since Lydia had come into her life. Until now.

The feelings all but choked her, until Jack finally spoke. "No, we're putting distance between us and whoever is after you. We'll stop when I think it's safe."

Ali was shocked that just words, any words at all from Jack, began to dispel those old feelings, allowing her to focus on the present. On the Terrines. On the fact that someone tried to kill her, and they'd try again. The past receded and she kept her eyes on Jack. "Will we be safe anywhere?"

"I can't guarantee it." He shrugged, a sharp movement in the shadows. "Hell, there aren't any guarantees in life."

She let go of the sides of the seat and wrapped her arms around herself. "There sure aren't."

He glanced at her briefly. "Did you really think that you could be with someone like Mick Terrine and have a fairy-tale ending?"

"I know there aren't any fairy-tale endings in this world." She sank back in the seat and turned to the night. Finding Lydia and finding a real home, after all the temporary places she and Alicia had been assigned to, was as close to a fairy-tale ending as she'd ever found. And now that was all disintegrating before her eyes. "Mick Terrine has nothing to do with that."

Jack had a hard time concentrating on his driving when Ali was talking. And if her voice hadn't been touched by a certain sadness, he would have felt better. If he hadn't wanted to reach out and take her hand, to try to banish that sadness, he would have felt a whole lot better.

Will hadn't told him anything about her background beyond her relationship with Terrine, and he found himself wondering how she had become the woman she was now. An agonizing combination of beauty, sensuality, sadness and...stupidity. "Are you from this area?" he asked.

"No. California."

"My old stomping grounds. Northern or Southern?"

"Mostly Southern California."

"Where, exactly?"

She didn't speak for a moment, then recited in a flat tone, "L.A., Pasadena, Santa Monica, Burbank, Van Nuys, Torrence, Seal Beach...and Compton." She exhaled, the sound a sigh in the confines of the Jeep. "I don't remember the other places exactly."

"Your family moved around a lot?"

He knew she'd turned to face him, but he kept his eyes on the road ahead. "No. Those are the cities that the Los Angeles County Foster Child Program covered.''

"What?"

"I was orphaned when I was five, and I was in and out of a lot of foster homes in L.A. County."

No fairy-tale endings there, thought Jack. No wonder she'd wound up with a man like Terrine. She probably thought he had money and influence, that she'd have a lot of things she'd never had before. What a bad mistake. "How did you end up coming to Las Vegas?"

He heard her shift and he could feel her moving a bit farther from him. Oddly, he didn't like that. "It seemed like the thing to do."

"You dealt blackjack?"

"For a while."

"Is that how you met Terrine?"

"I really don't want to talk about...about this. Can't we talk about something else?"

Jack wished he could ask her if she honestly thought Mick Terrine could have been her Prince Charming. But the idea of her with that man was leaving a distinctly bitter taste at the back of his tongue. He didn't fight a change of direction in their talk. "Name a subject."

"You."

"Me?"

"Why not? I've often wondered why people go into law enforcement. I never thought they could pay people enough to put their lives on the line all the time."

"A cop doesn't think like that." He stopped himself. He had. Five years ago. His hands tightened on the steering wheel. "At least, they can't if they want to be good at what they do."

"Why?"

"Once a cop thinks about his own mortality, he tightens up. He thinks before he acts, and in a life-and-death situation, you have to live by your instincts. If he can't, he's more of a liability than an asset."

"Is that why you're quitting?"

It almost angered him that she saw through him so easily, almost as much as it angered him that he was telling this woman things he had hardly sorted through in his own mind. He answered with a partial truth. "I've done all I can do as a cop."

"How do you know that?"

She wouldn't let up. "Listen, I've been around cops all my life. My father, grandfather and both brothers have been or are, cops. Believe me, I can do more good prosecuting than bringing crooks in, then watching them walk away because of a legal slipup or a glitch in the law."

"Like what happened with Mick before?"

God, she was a damned mind reader. "Yeah, I guess so."

"What happened when he hit you with the tire iron?"

"Do you want the physical sensations or the mental ones?"

"Both."

He sighed. "Physically, it felt like I'd been run over by a ten-ton truck. I literally saw stars. I bet you didn't know that really happens, but it does. Then he caught my shoulder. That felt as if I'd hit a cement wall going eighty miles an hour. And there was blood all over."

He could feel her staring at him, and he found himself almost laughing. "I survived. But it made me furious that the man walked away from it."

"But he injured you."

"Self-defense."

"What?"

"That's what he pleaded, and given the circumstances, the judge bought it." He fingered the steering wheel, eyes fixed on the dark road. "Emotionally, I was filled with anger and frustration, and that doesn't make for an attractive cop."

"So you decided to drop out?"

He hated that expression. "No. I was going to law school part-time, I just stepped it up and graduated six months ago. Now I just have to pass the bar exams."

"And I'm keeping you from studying."

"As a matter of fact, you are—you and Mick Terrine."

He knew he'd rebuffed her, yet it was the truth. When she spoke again, she changed the subject slightly. "How long have you been on the police force?"

"Thirteen years."

"Lucky thirteen?"

That brought a burst of laughter from him. "Maybe so, and maybe I'll pass the bar."

"How did you get pulled into this?"

He was asking himself the same thing, especially since the shooting and he was facing losing the whole weekend. "It's a favor for a friend."

"The man at the courthouse?"

He cast her a quick look and saw she was leaning against the door and partially facing him. "Yeah, we go back a long way. I owed him."

Again she changed the direction of the conversation. "Why don't you go into private practice?"

"Why would I?"

"There isn't much money in the district attorney's office, is there?"

The crux of the matter, and maybe the crux of the relationship she had with Terrine. An orphan shifted from place to place, and she finally found someone she thought could give her what she'd never had. "And money solves everything?"

"No, but I'm sure it helps."

"Answer me something."

"What?"

"If the Terrines had offered you money for your silence, would you have taken it?" When she hesitated, he felt his heart tighten. He was used to dealing with criminals, people who seldom spoke without weighing every word for effect, and it seemed Ali was doing that very thing right now.

She pressed into the corner by the door, hugging herself tightly, her fingers digging into her upper arms. Questions meant to fill the void, to distract her and to let her know more about this man had taken a wrong turn, right back to the Terrines.

Now she had to ask herself if Alicia would have taken money, then walked away? Could she have been bought? Had Terrine tried? Before all this happened, Ali would have said Alicia couldn't have been bought. Her sister was a free spirit, someone who couldn't be confined, who seldom trusted others, but she was a woman who was honest. Now Ali didn't know. She would have never thought Alicia could have been close to a man like Mick Terrine.

Her head was beginning to throb, and she wished she could just tell Jack the truth, that she wasn't Alicia, that Alicia was in Los Angeles. But she knew that, as soon as the police knew where Alicia was, they'd go after her. If they went after her, the Terrines wouldn't be far behind.

"How much would it have taken for you to walk away and never look back?" Jack persisted.

She flinched at the edge to his voice and realized there was no way she could tell him the truth. There was far too much at stake. "I said I didn't want to talk about this," she managed. "Are our things in the car?"

"Everything we had at the hotel."

She turned away from Jack, leaning her shoulder against the door and touching her cheek to the coolness of the glass. The moon was high in the sky now, bathing the desert in an eerie light where nothing had color, just darks and lights. Gray, all shades of gray.

She glanced at the clock in the dash. The glowing green digits read 10:50. They'd been driving for almost three hours, and it had been much longer since she'd tried to eat. She felt tired, and hunger gnawed at her stomach. And she couldn't stand the silence any longer. "Can we listen to the radio?"

Without a word, Jack flipped it on, fiddled with the dial, and country music drifted into the car, the reception touched by faint static. Anything was better than the silence. "You like country—"

"Listen," Jack said.

Ali looked at him and saw he was staring at the radio. "What?"

"Can't you hear that?"

"Hear what?"

Jack suddenly pulled off the road and into the parking lot of a truck stop. "Are we going to stay here?" she asked, sitting straighter and looking at the glaring lights from a diner, gas station and a shabby-looking motel.

"No." Jack stopped near a series of big rigs parked and idling and got out. Ali twisted in the seat to watch him move around the Jeep, bending over, feeling under the bumper, the fenders at the front. Then he called to Ali, "Pull the hood release."

She stretched across the seat to look around under the dash, then saw the lever. She tugged on it, then sat up and saw Jack lift the hood. He was out of sight for a moment, then the hood crashed down and he came around to her side of the Jeep. Ali rolled down the window and watched him.

Jack dropped to his knees and looked under the car. He inched his hand along the bottom of the frame. Suddenly he pulled his hand back. He stood up and came to the window, a tiny silver circular object in his hand. It was no bigger than a dime, and maybe twice as thick. "We've got company," he said. "We're bugged."

Ali stared at the tiny piece of metal. "You mean—"

"Someone's got us on their screen, following us, waiting until they've got a clear view." Suddenly Jack smiled, the humor pure and deep in his eyes. "Let's give them a ride."

Ali watched him head toward the cab of the closest big rig, then look right and left. Quickly he pushed his hand under a lip of metal near one of the front wheels, then came back to the Jeep, went around and climbed in. "That truck's going to Oklahoma. I hope Terrine's men like that area."

Ali almost laughed at the idea of the bad guys chasing the truck into Oklahoma. Then she sobered. They would know she and Jack weren't heading that way. But how long would it take for them to know they'd been had?

Chapter 6

"This looks good," Jack said an hour later.

Ali sat up, saw the glow of building lights coming out of the night, and the next thing she knew, they were pulling off the highway into the parking lot of a restaurant and motel. They passed a garish pink neon sign on top of a twenty-foot pole by the road that read Charlie's Palace. A smaller green sign below it flashed Vacancy on and off.

Jack pulled to the right of the restaurant and stopped in front of the first motel unit, which had a red neon sign—Manager's Office—in the window. He looked at Ali. "Sit tight. I'll be right back."

As he got out and disappeared into the office, Ali glanced at the other motel units. A scattering of cars were parked in front of them, and in some of them she could see the blue flickering of televisions behind curtains. Age and disrepair were everywhere, from the dull wood siding to the sagging steps that led up to each unit, and the sloping roof that looked as if it came straight out of the fifties.

Jack came back out and got into the Jeep. As he started it and put it into gear, he said, "We've got the room at the far end. I can park the Jeep behind it and keep it out of sight."

As he headed toward the last door, Ali realized what he said. "*We* have a room?"

He drove past the unit, rounded the corner and pulled the Jeep to a stop along the side wall. He shifted to look at Ali, his right hand touching the back of her seat. "One room. The idea is that I don't let you out of my sight. I can't do that with a wall between us."

It didn't matter that Ali wished she had a brick wall two feet thick between herself and this man; she couldn't argue with his logic. "Of course not," she murmured, reaching for the door handle.

She followed him back around to the front. The unit at one time had been number twenty-eight, but now the two was a faded spot on the dull brown door, and the eight was tarnished brass. Jack pushed the key into the lock, then stood back to let Ali go first into the darkened room, which smelled of age and disinfectant.

He snapped on a light and exposed a room with wallpaper that must once have been a warm gold and beige, but now was faded to a brownish blur, its pattern indecipherable. A single white globe hung from a low ceiling discolored by water leaks, and the carpet, in a shade that closely approximated the color of dead grass, was threadbare.

Ali went farther inside while Jack closed the door. She understood one room. She understood the need to stay close. What she didn't understand was one bed, a king-size bed that sagged in the middle, took up most of the space and was covered in a beige chenille spread.

She felt the room getting close, the air getting less available. Being alone with Jack this weekend was one thing, and being in this room with him was inescapable, but she knew there was no way she could share his bed.

Jack watched Ali and he could almost read her mind. One bed. He knew how he'd felt when the man in the office had said that was the best he could do. There weren't any rooms with two beds available that allowed easy access to the Jeep while it was kept out of sight. And to be honest, he wished they could have had rooms at opposite ends of the motel, but things didn't work out the way he wanted. They hadn't for a long time.

Before Ali could say anything, he went around her to the open bathroom door at the far side of the room. He snapped on the light, saw the small shower stall, toilet and sink, then turned and met Ali's gaze. Damn it, he hated it when she had that look, as if a light breeze could lift her right off her feet. He didn't want to be touched by her on any level. Even before that thought was completed, he knew it was too late to hope for that.

Instead, he just needed to keep this on a professional footing. He was the protector, and she was the target he was protecting. Simple. Sure, and so was the theory of relativity. All he knew for certain was he needed distance, some space for a few minutes to get his bearings.

"There's only one bed," she said, a telltale blush staining her cheeks.

Jack moved quickly, talking as he headed for escape. "That's all they had. I need to call in right now. Lock the door after me and don't open it for anyone. I've got a key."

When he was passing her and just inches from a clean escape, she reached out and touched his arm. It stopped him in his tracks. He looked down at her hand where it rested on his sleeve, then made himself look at her upturned face.

"You aren't leaving, are you?" she asked, her voice unsteady, the same faint trembling he could feel in her touch.

"I have to call in."

She looked around, then let go of him to cross to the phone sitting on the bedside table. "Here, use this," she said, lifting the receiver and holding it out.

"No. I can't take a chance of the call being traced." He went to the door, but looked back to find Ali still by the bed, the phone receiver dangling from her hand at her side. "Lock the door. I'll be right back."

As the door closed behind Jack, Ali hurried across to push the lock in on the knob. She turned to the empty room, then slowly went to the bed and dropped onto the edge. Staring at the phone, she wanted nothing more than to call the hospital and talk to Lydia. She wanted to find out if Alicia got there, how Lydia was doing, anything to touch base with a life she understood. But she couldn't do that any more than she could admit the truth to Jack.

Totally alone, Ali felt tears prick her eyes. Damn it, she never cried. She'd learned a long time ago that tears just didn't make a difference in this life. They hadn't stopped the moves from foster home to foster home, or stopped Alicia and her from being separated for months at a time, or stopped Lydia from getting sick. And they wouldn't change anything now.

But she couldn't prevent the tears from slipping from her eyes. She couldn't prevent the sobs as she rolled onto her side or that heavy feeling of being disoriented and afraid. She pulled her knees to her stomach and closed her eyes tightly. Damn it, why did her only link to sanity right now have to be a man with blue eyes that could fill with real hatred for her at the mention of the name Terrine?

Jack could see the door to the room from the pay phones by the manager's office. He put the call through to Will's home, and when his friend came on the line, Jack spoke quickly. "We've landed, but we had a passenger."

"What?"

"I took care of it. He got off about eighty miles back and I think he's heading east. Right now, everything looks clear."

"Try to keep it that way."

"Same to you." He knew he should hang up as soon as he could, but he found himself asking Will, "Did you ever find out what the truth is about her relationship with the man?"

Will was silent, then he said, "Does it matter?"

It shouldn't, Jack knew, yet in some way he couldn't begin to define it did. "No, I'm just curious."

"Let's put it this way—that type of man doesn't keep a girl on the hook to look good. He uses her."

Jack closed his eyes for a moment, then said, "Yeah, you're right."

"I won't expect to hear from you again until Monday."

"Right," Jack said, and put the receiver back in the cradle. He stood staring at the closed door at the far end of the motel, then with a low violent oath that echoed a frustration that had been growing in him since he'd taken over this job, he went out into the night. He stopped by the vending machines by the office, got some cookies, chips and two cans of soda, then headed back to the room.

Jack slipped back into the room with his key, relocked the door, then turned to see Ali on the bed. She was asleep, curled up into a ball like a small child trying to protect herself. As he moved closer to the bed, he saw that her face, partially veiled by her loose hair, was streaked with mascara, the dampness clinging to her cheeks.

It shook him to realize she'd been crying. Having a lover turn on you had to be frightening; having that lover want you dead had to be devastating.

Ali stirred, took a shuddering breath, then settled back into the fetal position, her hands clenched into fists by her cheeks. In that moment he felt a wave of genuine protectiveness wash over him, but it had little to do with her value as a witness. It was her, this woman he was no more than two feet from. This woman who touched the air around him with a gentle sweetness, this woman who had looked scared to death when he'd left the room earlier.

When she moaned softly, he turned from her, dropped the snacks on the bedside table, then crossed to the bathroom. He went in and closed the door, then ran cool water and splashed his face with it. He gripped the edge of the sink with both hands and looked at himself in the mottled mirror. "And you were going to study all weekend," he muttered at his reflection.

"Jack? Jack?"

The sound of Ali's calling his name jarred him, and he reached for the door. When he opened it, he saw Ali in the middle of the bed on her knees, her hair tumbling wildly around her tearstained face. "Jack?"

"I'm here," he said as he hurried toward the bed.

"Thank God," she breathed as she sank back on her heels. "I heard a sound, and I..." She shook her head. "I didn't hear you come in, and I...I guess I'm nervous."

"So am I," he admitted as he stood over her by the bed. When she looked at him as if she didn't believe him, he sank down on the side of the bed. "You don't have a corner on being nervous about what can happen."

It wasn't a lover of his who was trying to kill him, but Terrine had left his mark. He didn't have to touch the scar to remember. He saw Ali take a shuddering breath and impulsively reached out to touch the hand that was clenched on her thigh.

She twisted her hand under his, and the next thing he knew, her fingers were laced tightly with his, her other hand on top of his. "They can't find us, can they?" she asked intently.

He was shocked at the smallness of her hands holding his, and his first impulse was to lie to her, to tell her that they were safe, that nothing bad could ever happen to her while she was with him. But he couldn't. Lies and false assurances wouldn't help anything.

"I told you before there aren't any guarantees. For now, we're safe. But we can only stay here for a while to get some sleep, then we'll move on." He tried to smile, to take the edge off the tension that surrounded both of them. "And right now, I need my hand back."

She looked down at her hands holding his, then drew back abruptly. "I . . . I'm sorry."

He hated himself for doing that. He hated the feeling of emptiness now that she wasn't touching him. And he hated himself for feeling that way. He stood and looked at the low overstuffed chair near the window. "You take the bed."

"What about you?" she asked.

"I'll be over there," he said, motioning to the chair.

"No, I'll take the chair," she said. "You need to rest, and you can't in the chair." She scrambled off the bed. "I can sleep anywhere."

"So can I. I've slept standing up before."

She looked at the chair, then back at him and said quickly, "We could share the bed. It's big enough for two."

"No," he said without hesitating, the idea of lying in bed with this woman as unthinkable as the idea that kept flitting around the edges of his mind—that she was inordinately attractive even without makeup and flashy clothes. Lying next to her and trying to pretend she was just another case was ludicrous at best. And it would be impossible.

She frowned at him, a tiny line tugging between her wide eyes. "You don't want to be that close to anyone who had anything to do with Mick Terrine, do you?"

For a flashing instant, Jack had a mental image of Ali with Terrine, her face flushed with passion, her lips swollen from kisses, her— He shook his head sharply. "It's not that," he lied, shocked at how easily the lie came to his lips and how right she was.

"I'm not asking you to sleep *with* me, just near me," she said, color rising in her face, accentuating the mascara smudges and erasing her former paleness. "I just thought we both needed our sleep." She shook her head, her hair drifting around her shoulders. "Never mind. Believe me, I wasn't trying to seduce you."

His stomach clenched and he swallowed quickly. Seduce him? That conjured up images he couldn't begin to contend with. "I didn't say that. It's just not—"

She moved abruptly, speaking as she padded toward the bathroom. "I've got an idea. We both need the bed. Did you ever watch the movie *It Happened One Night* with Clark Gable and—"

"Claudette Colbert. I know the movie," he cut in as she tugged open the sliding closet door by the bathroom. "And don't tell me you want me to string up a blanket to divide the bed in two."

"No," she said as she reached inside the closet, took out a stack of blankets and came back to the bed. She shook them out, then methodically began to roll them up the way someone would carpeting. "The Walls of Jericho don't have to come down," she said pushing the roll of blankets into the middle of the bed. "They can also lie down."

He didn't say anything while she lay the roll right down the middle, then sank back on her heels and looked at him. A smile came without warning, lifting the corners of her pale lips and touching her eyes with light. It made Jack blink the way a flood of bright sunlight would have after a storm. She gestured toward the pillows with her hands, palms up.

"Presto. The Walls of Jericho. Completely safe, and more comfortable than the chair." More comfortable, he'd concede, but he wasn't so sure about the "safe."

Ali watched Jack, not willing to admit that she just wanted someone close. She didn't want to be alone in the dark, the feelings a throwback to her childhood when she couldn't sleep without Alicia beside her and the lights on. Right now the idea of being isolated in the darkness was too much to contemplate.

She looked away from Jack, knowing her smile wouldn't hold, and smoothed the rolled-up blankets with both hands. "It would work just fine, just like two twin beds. A long time ago, they did this. They used to call it 'bundling,' so a man and a woman could sleep in the same bed safely." She was babbling as she adjusted the ridge down the center of the bed, but didn't dare stop in case she found herself begging Jack to do it. "Sometimes it was a wooden divider, a long plank nailed at the headboard and footboard and sometimes a foot high. Sometimes it was a rolled-up blanket like this or a specially made long pillow filled with down feathers. The wooden plank—"

"Ali," Jack said, stopping her words.

Her hands stilled, but she didn't look at him. Ever since she'd met him, she'd had the most disconcerting feeling that he could see into her mind and read her thoughts. And she didn't want to take that chance this time. She stared at the roll of blankets, her hands still on them. "What?"

"You've made your point. A barrier is a barrier."

She looked up as he crossed to wedge a straight-backed chair under the handle of the door. Then he turned. "I'll take the side by the door." He pointed to the nightstand. "I know you're picky about what you eat, but I bought some stuff at the machines outside. You didn't eat a thing at dinner, so help yourself."

Ali saw the junk food and almost laughed. To her, it looked like a feast fit for a king. "Beggars can't be choosers," she said as she reached for a can of soda and a bag of chips. Jack sat down on the edge of the bed and slipped off his shoes and socks. "Don't you want something?" she asked as she popped the tab on the soda. "After all..."

Her words trailed off as Jack stood and tugged the sweatshirt over his head. His chest was exposed, the hard muscles that rippled at his abdomen, the dusting of sandy brown hair that feathered in a suggestive T across his pectorals and down to disappear into the waist of his jeans. The sight made her mouth go dry, and as he tossed the sweatshirt at the chair, Ali saw the scar. The scar a tire iron had made.

It marred the smoothness of his skin at the top of his shoulder and cut jaggedly down his biceps almost to his elbow. Even though he'd been damaged by it, it didn't distract from a maleness that seemed to hover around him like a cloak. Ali made herself look away and take a gulp of soda.

She coughed when some of the carbonated beverage went down the wrong way. Then she scrambled off the bed and headed for the bathroom. "I'll be right back," she managed, then went into the small room and closed the door. But just shutting the door couldn't shut out the memory of Jack stripping off his shirt. And it couldn't nullify the reaction she'd had to the sight.

She put the soda on the side of the sink, then washed her face and rinsed out her mouth. When she looked at herself in the mirror, she tried to figure out how the person she'd been just a day ago could have disappeared so completely. The Alison Sullivan who had left Los Angeles for Las Vegas had been sure of what she wanted in life, quiet, not impulsive. Diametrically opposite of her twin. Now she knew just how close she was to being Alicia.

She was in a motel with a stranger, experiencing feelings so new to her they scared her, and she was running for her life. Either she had finally entered the real world, or she was like the fairy-tale Alice falling into Wonderland.

Brushing her hair back from her face, she muttered at her reflection, "Get a grip."

She finished her soda, then tossed the can into the wastebasket and went back into the bedroom. Jack was on the far side of the bed, leaning against the headboard, a can of soda in his hand. "Feel better?" he asked.

She didn't meet his eyes and barely covered a yawn. "How long can we stay here?" she asked as she went to the bed.

"A few hours. We should be out of here no later than three or four, so you'd better get some sleep."

She didn't need to be encouraged to rest. She tugged back the blankets on her side, then without taking off anything but her shoes, crawled into bed. She shifted to lie with her back to Jack, bunched the pillow under her head. Then she felt the bed shift and knew Jack had gotten up. The next thing she knew, the room was plunged into complete darkness.

She sat bolt upright, not able to see a thing. "What are you doing?"

"I just turned out the lights," Jack said, his voice coming to her through the shadows.

"No, please, I..." She strained to make out something, anything in the darkness, and felt foolish. "I'm sorry. I can't sleep without a light on."

She heard him move, then the small light on her side of the bed snapped on. Jack was over her, back in the shadows, outside of the ring of light. "How's that?" he asked.

"I'm sorry. It's just that I...I..."

He moved away and around the bed. "No problem," he said, and she felt the bed shift again. "Just sleep. I'll wake you when it's time to go."

She sank back down and tugged the blankets up to her chin. "I'm used to sleeping with a light on," she said, needing to explain. "It's just a habit of mine."

"It's no problem. I can sleep in broad daylight. Nothing bothers me."

That sounded like paradise. Nothing to bother you. Nothing to keep sleep from coming. "In the foster homes, you couldn't keep a light on." She found herself explaining further. "It wasted money. And wasting money wasn't allowed."

"And it wasn't allowed to be afraid?" Jack asked softly.

He was too close to the truth of her past. "No, it wasn't." Not until Lydia. The thought of her foster mother brought the tears awfully close to the surface. "Good night," she said quickly.

"Good night, Ali," he said through the shadows.

She closed her eyes and rolled onto her side again, away from Jack.

Jack awoke with a start to a thin stream of gray light slanting across his closed eyes. He lay still, getting his bearings, then as he felt softness and heat against him, he knew everything. The Walls of Jericho had fallen sometime during the night.

He eased his eyes open, averting them from the gray light of dawn invading the room. A sleep that was supposed to have been for only a few hours had stretched to dawn, and the barrier of the rolled blankets hadn't been a barrier at all.

He could feel Ali against him. His arm was around her, her head resting in the hollow of his shoulder, and her hair was tickling his chin. Her leg lay over his thigh, her hand rested palm down on his chest, and he could feel every breath she took.

And he couldn't breathe. He felt her softness and curves, the way her breasts pressed against his side, the faint beating of her heart, the heat of her hand on his bare chest. She was curled into his side like a trusting child, but the way he was beginning to respond was not anything he'd ever felt for a child.

His body was tensing, blood rushing through his veins, and he was sure that he'd lost the ability to take one more deep breath. Yet at the same time he felt a sense of peace that was staggering. He felt as if the world had been pushed away, forced outside the confines of this room, and what he was experiencing was something he'd been looking for all his life.

What a joke, he thought. Lust was lust. That was it. To be blunt, he was sexually aroused by a woman who probably had the same effect on every man she met. A lot of men felt this surge of desire mixed with tenderness. A lot of men had lain with her, felt her snuggle into their side and felt the need to stay with her forever. Maybe Mick Terrine had no intention of forever, but he sure as hell had known the lust and need.

The thought of Terrine brought everything into perspective, and Jack only wanted to get away. Carefully he tried to ease away from her, to free his arm and shift her off his shoulder. But before he could escape, she stirred. In the low light from the lamp and the grayness of dawn, he looked down at Ali, saw her eyelids flutter and her lips part softly as if anticipating a kiss.

Jack froze, then as her tongue touched her lips, he felt as if he was fragmenting, the desire surging back with such intensity it made him light-headed. Her hand moved on the bare skin of his chest, softly skimming upward to rest at the base of his throat. She sighed softly, her lashes fluttered again, and for an instant he was looking into the sleepy green depths of her eyes.

An unsettling impulse, the culmination of what he'd felt since the first time he'd been close to her outside the rest room in the courthouse, possessed him. He lowered his head, and as soon as the silky softness and heat of her lips touched him, a bolt of pure wanting shot through him. There was a hunger in him that he'd never known before, a sense of incompleteness that startled him and confused him.

He wanted to hold her, mold her to him, let the hot spots of awareness where her body made contact with his flare into flame. And when he felt her shift, her hand slide around his shoulders, her mouth mold to his, her taste and breath mingle with his, he didn't dare move. A fire could rage in a heartbeat. He could take her here and now, and possess her as he had no other woman he'd ever been with. And the idea made him ache.

The kiss deepened, his tongue tasting her, tracing the smooth ridge of her teeth, entwining with her tongue, and he felt as if he could almost inhale her sigh into his soul. His hand lifted, slipping under her tangle of curls to cup the nape of her neck. His thumb felt the erratic pulse at the sensitive spot below her ear. And the rhythm echoed his own.

As she arched toward him, her breasts pressed to his chest, he almost pulled her closer, so that there would be nothing between them at all. But in that moment, he realized what a staggering mistake he was making. Nothing between them? There was no conceivable way he could call Mick Terrine nothing.

And the man had been even closer to Ali than this. He'd known her in a way that made Jack feel as if he had been hit in the gut. He drew back and found himself looking down at Ali, her hair a brilliant halo on the white cotton pillowcase, her eyes wide with shock. It looked for all the world as if she was just as stunned by what had happened as he was, yet she shouldn't have been. It was her idea to share the bed.

He steeled himself as he let her go, shifting back on the bed. As far as he was concerned, she was just one step above Terrine, and maybe that innocent act was the very thing Terrine found so appealing about her. Maybe that was the weapon that had gotten him hooked. It sure as hell had worked on him.

Jack felt as if he'd been blindsided and almost inducted into a huge fraternity, and not a terribly distinguished one—men who'd slept with this woman.

He saw color rise in her face and her lashes sweep low to partially veil the green depths of her eyes. And his desire for her was still there, settling into a deep frustrated ache. He exhaled in a rush and knew he had to put emotional and physical distance between this woman and himself, between her and his own stupidity.

He turned from her, then threw his legs over the side of the bed and stood. He ran both hands over his face, then reached for the gun in the snap holster on the nightstand. He pushed the clip onto the waistband of his jeans, averting his eyes from the evidence of just how much he'd wanted her physically. And as he turned to Ali there was no way to deny what had almost happened.

Trying to control a growing sickness deep in his be-ing, he saw her sitting up, her knees drawn to her breasts, her arms holding tightly to them. Her eyes were averted, staring at the mussed sheet and blan-kets around her bare feet.

Without those green eyes meeting his gaze, he could form coherent thoughts. She used to awaken in Mick Terrine's arms and make love with him. And now she was willing to hold on to Jack. The phrase "any port in a storm" came to his mind and helped him steel himself against the memory of her taste and touch. "That wouldn't make any difference," he said, his voice edged with a hardness that only reflected his need to steel himself against her.

She pressed her forehead to her knees. "What wouldn't?" she asked in a low muffled voice.

"You don't have to do anything for me to do my job." As the words came out, he realized that was ex-actly what he thought. It was exactly what made that dull ache settle behind his breastbone and grow as she lifted her head and finally met his gaze. "I don't take bribes."

She paled, her eyes narrowing as if she wanted to avoid looking right at him. The silence in the room was deafening, lasting for what felt like an eternity before she turned away and got off the bed. She walked to the bathroom, stopped, then, staring at the floor, said softly, "And I don't give bribes." Then she turned and went inside, closing the door with a soft click.

If she had screamed at him or slammed the door, Jack would have salvaged some satisfaction from what he'd said. Instead, he felt as if he'd been struck in the stomach, as if he'd abused her in some way he couldn't begin to understand. With a low oath, he raked his hand across his mouth, desperate to get the feel and taste of her off his lips, then he moved to the window. He shifted the curtains enough to see outside, and when he didn't see anyone, he crossed the room, grabbed his sweatshirt and pulled it on.

He walked to the door, jerked the chair out from under the knob, shoved it to one side, then unlocked the door and stepped out into the heat of the morning. He squinted at the brilliance of the rising sun bouncing off the desert all around and felt as if mistakes were piling up on him. From the first moment he'd agreed to do this to the moment he'd kissed her. Mistakes.

He'd be damned if he'd make any more mistakes.

Chapter 7

As Ali stood under the warm running water, the moment when she'd awakened, felt arms around her, heat at her side and a heartbeat under her palm dissolved into a memory she wasn't sure had been real.

She closed her eyes and leaned against the tiles of the shower stall. One minute she'd been falling asleep, trying to forget why she was in the motel, the next she'd been in Jack's arms, feeling safe and grounded. An illusion. The way the kiss had been an illusion. It had excited her and frightened her at the same time. Then the connection had been gone, coldness had been all around, and Jack had looked at her with disgust.

She reached for the faucet, turned it off, then stepped out of the shower and grabbed a towel. As she wrapped it around her, she saw herself in the mirror over the sink. Huge shadowed eyes, pale skin and tightness at her mouth. She looked lost and alone, yet just moments ago she'd felt the heat of bare male skin under her hands, tasted the essence of a man with her tongue and lips, and had let an illusion of the right-ness of being where she was wash over her.

She reached for another towel and wrapped it tur-ban-style around her wet hair. And Jack had thought she was coming on to him, trying to bribe him. She swallowed the bitterness on the back of her tongue and turned from her reflection. *Get dressed, get out of here and put this weekend behind you,* she thought. She reached for the door and opened it a crack. She could see the bed, Alicia's blue suitcase lying on it beside Jack's big leather bag, but from what she could see the room was empty.

She stepped out, softly called, "Jack?" Nothing. She looked around, then saw the door was unlocked and the chair lying crookedly against the wall. And for an instant she knew pure terror. They'd found her.

Ali hurried across the room to the window and carefully looked out. She didn't realize just how scared she was until she saw Jack at the pay phone. Her nerves felt raw and exposed, and she had to take a moment to breathe—in through her nose, out through her mouth—before she felt settled enough to go to the suitcase and pull out some clean clothes.

Then she went back to the bathroom and quickly donned yellow shorts, a white T-shirt and leather thong sandals. She skimmed her damp hair back off her face and caught it in a clip at the nape of her neck. She didn't bother with makeup.

She returned to the bedroom and packed her things. Just as she closed the suitcase, the door opened. She turned to ask Jack if they were leaving, but the words never came out.

Jack burst into the room, barely pausing to grab his bag from the bed. "We have to leave. Now. Someone's been around looking for you." He talked quickly as he checked the bathroom, then came back into the bedroom. "Damn it, we shouldn't have stayed so long. I never—" He cut off his own words as he looked at Ali. "Have you got everything?"

"Yes, but how do you know they've been around?"

He pulled a folded paper out of the pocket of his jeans and held it out to her. "I saw this in the manager's office when I went in to get change for the phone."

Ali unfolded the white paper and looked down at a grainy black-and-white copy of a photo of Alicia. Her sister was in a bikini, standing by a pool, smiling into the camera. "How . . . how did you get it?"

As she looked up, he headed for the door. "It was on the desk. I grabbed it. Now, come on. We're out of here, now."

Jack could feel his heart hammering against his ribs. And that fear was pushing him off center. He knew when he went back to the room and saw Ali that it wasn't entirely a fear of being found that scared him. It was what could happen to Ali. It scared him to death to think of how close Terrine's men must have been to her while he slept. Or still were.

He looked at her, her hair pulled back off her face, her makeup gone, exposing a face of translucent beauty. He felt fear choke him as he turned and opened the door just enough to get a clear view of the

FIND OUT <u>INSTANTLY</u> IF YOU GET UP TO 5 FREE GIFTS IN THE

CARNIVAL WHEEL

▼ **SCRATCH-OFF GAME!** ▼

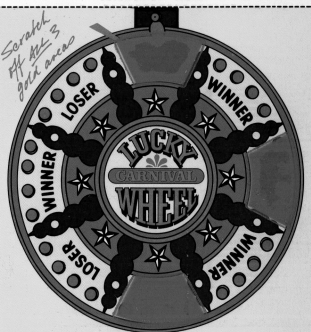

YES! I have scratched off the 3 Gold Areas above. Please send me all the gifts for which I qualify. I understand I am under no obligation to purchase any books, as explained on the opposite page.

245 CIS AG46
(U-SIL-IM-01/93)

NAME

ADDRESS   APT.

CITY   STATE   ZIP

DETACH AND MAIL CARD TODAY!

BUSINESS REPLY MAIL
FIRST CLASS MAIL   PERMIT NO. 717   BUFFALO, NY

POSTAGE WILL BE PAID BY ADDRESSEE

SILHOUETTE READER SERVICE
3010 WALDEN AVE
PO BOX 1867
BUFFALO NY 14240-9952

NO POSTAGE
NECESSARY
IF MAILED
IN THE
UNITED STATES

parking lot and highway beyond. Nothing looked out of place.

"I'll get the Jeep, bring it around, and when I come even with the door, get in and get down."

Without waiting for her to say anything, he picked up both suitcases and her purse, then with a glance at her, he went out to the Jeep. He tossed the luggage into the back, got in and drove around to the front of the unit. The minute he stopped, Ali ran from the room, got in, and without having to be told, crouched on the floor by the seat, making herself completely invisible from the outside.

Oddly, it pleased him that she was smart enough to do that. Then again, it was her life. He put the Jeep into gear and drove slowly out of the parking lot and onto the highway. Heading north, he kept checking the rearview mirror.

The motel manager saw movement from the end unit, and as he looked out the office window, he saw a black Jeep stop and a slender woman with flame-red hair running toward it. He saw the plate and looked at the registration book. The plate number was different from the one in the book for that unit—the same numbers, but the driver had mixed them up, and the make had been entered as a Bronco.

As the Jeep drove past the office and out onto the road, he saw the driver. He didn't recognize him, but the register said Mr. and Mrs. Jeffers. Mrs. Jeffers with red hair. He looked for the picture the two men had brought in earlier. The bald man had said the woman had bright red hair. He shuffled through the mess of papers on his desk, but the picture wasn't there. Then he saw the small card with the phone number on it the bald man had handed to him with the picture.

He frowned as he reached for the phone. Kidnapping was a terrible thing, and after all, he could use the reward. He'd been wanting to go to Vegas again, get a job at one of the big hotels. If he got the five thousand dollars, he'd be able to go first-class for a while. He dialed the number, and as he tucked the card into his pocket, he heard a man answer, "Yes?"

"A couple of guys left your number with me in case I seen a woman they said was kidnapped."

"Yeah, what've you got?"

"I'm Morris Evans out at Charlie's Palace motel on Route 95. I think I just seen the woman."

Just when Ali's legs were beginning to ache from crouching in the front, Jack touched the seat by him. "Get comfortable. No one's following us."

She got onto the seat and felt the leather, hot from the morning sun, against the back of her bare legs. As Jack flicked the air conditioner on high, she sat back and gazed at the country around them. The desert baked in the sun, the line of low hills in the distance shimmering and dancing against the clear sky. "How did they know where we went?"

"They must have caught on to the Oklahoma decoy pretty fast, then kept going in the same direction." He adjusted the rearview mirror, checked both side mirrors, then said, "For now we're alone, but it won't last."

She darted a nervous look out the back window, at cars that seemed innocuous, but then again, she had no idea what kind of car a killer might drive. She looked at Jack. "What are we going to do?"

"Disappear," he said succinctly.

She frowned. "That's what I thought we were doing when we left Las Vegas, but they got awfully close again."

"So, we attack it from a different angle."

"What angle?"

"What do you do when a person knows what to look for?"

She leaned a shoulder against the coolness of the door and studied Jack. "I don't know, what do you do, officer?"

"You give them something they aren't looking for." He was talking in riddles. "You make the expected the unexpected."

"How?"

"What stands out about us? What do you think everyone will be looking for, besides your red hair?"

She welcomed the brush of cool air from the vents as it fanned her warm skin. "You?"

"No, I'm not the kind of person who stands out. Try again."

She thought how wrong he was. Jack wouldn't go unnoticed anywhere. "I give up. What?"

"This Jeep. We have to ditch it. If they could bug it, they sure as hell know all about it. When you were getting dressed, I called some car-rental places." He slanted her a look. "We need another car, and I don't intend to steal one unless I'm forced to." She saw a hint of a smile that eased the brackets at his mouth. "Check in the glove compartment. There's an envelope in there with money in it. It won't be enough to buy a car, but it should be enough to rent one."

Ali snapped open the glove compartment and took out a brown envelope. Opening it, she looked inside and found another envelope. She took it out, opened it and found a stack of bills. Carefully she counted them. "A thousand dollars." She put them back into the smaller envelope. "Can you rent a car without a credit card?"

"I'll leave a security deposit. I've got ID, so it won't be a problem." He flipped down the sun visor and slipped something out of a leather slot, which he handed to Ali.

She looked down at a California driver's license. It had Jack's picture on it, an old picture, but the scar evident on his chin. The name on it was Paul Jeffers, the address in San Diego. The statistics were cut and dried. The birth date would make Jack almost forty, his weight one hundred and eighty, his height six feet and his hair and eye color brown and blue, respectively.

She turned it over and thought it looked legitimate. "This isn't really yours, is it?"

"No. It's a phony. Storm took care of it for me. We have IDs for emergencies that can be doctored up to look like they belong to whatever cops may have to belong to."

"Are you almost forty?"

"No, it just feels like that. I'll be thirty-six in six months. And that picture was taken about four years ago." She handed it back to him, and he tucked it into the slot on the sun visor. "But it'll do to get us through this if anyone wants ID."

"I thought people could get into all sorts of trouble for using phony IDs." Alicia had paid for a phony ID when she was sixteen so she could get into a dance club that wouldn't admit minors. It had worked, until one of the doormen recognized her. "I mean, that's illegal, isn't it?"

"Sure. But cops are resourceful. And they tend to be whatever it takes to do their job. Right now, we have to be the Jeffers." He swung off the main road and onto a narrow two-lane road that went east. "If I'm right, there's a town about ten miles down here called Marlow."

"What's in Marlow?" Ali asked.

"The car-rental place that said they'll take cash in lieu of a credit card."

"Why didn't the department just get you a phony credit card?"

"Too easy to trace, even one in a phony name."

"Live and learn," she murmured.

"That's what I'd hoped to be doing this weekend," he said, reminding her how everyone's lives had been disrupted in the past two days.

"You must be good friends to do this for..." She couldn't remember the other man's name.

"Will. And, yes, I owe him. If it wasn't for him, I'd be in jail for murder."

"What?"

He flashed her a smile, then looked back at the road. "I'm kidding. But I assure you I would have killed the junior Terrine if Will hadn't pulled me off him."

Ali almost wished he had killed the man five years ago. Then none of this would be happening. But as she looked at Jack, she realized she would have missed meeting him. And that seemed sad in a way. It didn't make sense to her, and she was saved from having to rationalize the thought when Jack spoke up.

"We're here. Marlow, Nevada."

Ali turned and saw a sign by the road—Marlow, Nevada, pop. 7,901. Just beyond she saw the buildings of a town centered around the highway and fanning out both north and south from the road with housing tracts, small industrial areas and businesses.

Marlow was like so many towns, innocuous, something you'd pass through and never really notice, unless you needed something. "We're looking for Rent Rite Rentals. They're on Blossom Springs Road. Keep an eye open for it."

Ali watched the streets go by, all of them named as if the city was a garden spot. Roses Lane, Elm Street, Sycamore Avenue, Cherry Lane. Yet the trees were few and far between, and flowers were almost nonexistent. Steel-walled stores, quonset-hut garages and flat-roofed houses lined the streets. Then Ali spotted their street. "Blossom Springs Road," she said, and pointed left.

Jack turned onto the street and halfway down the first block was a huge yellow sign for Rent Rite Rentals. He drove past the lot, which was partially filled with new-looking cars and a few vans, then made a U-turn and pulled into the curb a block away on the opposite side of the street. He stopped in the shade of a huge Eucalyptus tree that towered fifty feet in the air.

"Stay here. I'll take care of the rental. When I get out, move over to my seat, and when I stop beside you, get out and get into the rental as fast as you can."

He turned off the Jeep, took the keys out of the ignition and leaned across Ali's lap to snap open the glove compartment and toss the keys inside. She barely moved while he snapped it shut again, then sat back and looked at her.

"Lock the doors when you get out."

"Sure," she said.

He got out, reached back and grabbed the two suitcases, then paused to look in at her. "Keep your eyes open, and if anyone comes by, duck. I'll be back as fast as I can."

The door swung shut, and Jack walked quickly down the street to the rental place. Ali watched him disappear into a yellow building on one side of the lot. She moved across to the driver's seat, pulled her purse onto her lap and never took her eyes off the building. With the engine and air conditioner off, the Jeep soon got hot, and she could feel perspiration trickling between her breasts and down her back.

A car came down the street toward her, and Ali slipped low in the seat so she could just see over the dash. An elderly man and woman drove past, and Ali sat back up. She brushed at her still-damp hair and looked back at the yellow building. Right then the door opened and a man in a white shirt and blue slacks came out followed by Jack. The man handed Jack something, then went back inside.

Jack moved into the lot, stopped by a gray sedan and unlocked the door. He put the bags in back, then got in, and she watched as the car moved out of the lot and headed back up the street toward her. But when Jack got near, he turned away from the Jeep and drove off out of sight in the opposite direction.

Ali knew a moment of such pure panic that she thought she would die. He was leaving her. He'd driven off without a glance. She stared at the empty street, her hands gripping the steering wheel so tightly her fingers tingled. What was she supposed to do?

The keys. Jack had put them in the glove compartment. She shifted to reach for them, but stopped when she heard a car coming up from behind. Turning around, she almost cried with relief. The grey sedan was there, pulling alongside the Jeep. Ali scrambled out, grabbed her purse, hit the lock on the door, then slammed it.

Quickly she got into the sedan, into coolness, into a space where she wasn't alone, and dropped her purse on the floor at her feet. As she shut the door, Jack drove off, and Ali turned on him. "Why did you do that?" she demanded, her voice embarrassingly unsteady.

As Jack navigated toward the main street, he glanced at Ali with a frown. "Do what?"

"Just drive off, leave, then show up again!" She could barely take a breath. "Did you change your mind, or something?"

"Hey, cool down." Without warning, he touched her bare leg, his fingers pressing gently into her thigh. "I didn't *just* drive off. I was going around the block so when I got to you, the passenger door would be right by the driver's door to the Jeep. I also got a chance to scope out the territory to make sure there was no one watching who shouldn't be watching. It's part of my job."

She stared at his hand on her leg. God, he wasn't going to let her breathe one way or the other! And she felt stupid. Overreaction came to mind immediately, but she couldn't forget that horrible moment when she thought he'd abandoned her. Swallowing hard, she shifted on the seat, away from his touch, and he drew back to grip the steering wheel again as he turned onto the main street and headed east out of town.

"You . . . you should have told me."

"I didn't think I had to," he murmured.

"This might all be part of your job, but I don't know what you're doing."

"You're right. From now on, if you don't understand something, or it looks as if I've taken leave of my senses, just put up your hand and ask for an explanation. All right?"

"Sure," she muttered, pressing her shoulder against the door.

"I think we both need a bite to eat. Running from killers is always easier on a full stomach."

She glared at him, his humor falling horribly flat, but the idea of food was sort of appealing. All she'd had recently were the chips and soda he'd purchased at the motel vending machine. "Real food?"

"Real food," he repeated, and pointed ahead of them. "Burger in a basket. But I'm sure you can get a bowl of lettuce if we ask."

She exhaled, a smile threatening to tug up the corners of her lips. "I can handle a hamburger."

"You'll ingest meat?"

She did smile at that. "Just a bit. Well-done."

Jack smiled at her, the expression having almost as much impact as the moment he touched her leg. Damn it, it wasn't right for any man to look that good just because he smiled.

When Jack pulled into the drive-through of the fast-food restaurant, she concentrated on reading the menu, and by the time they pulled away, they both had double burgers, large fries and extra-large colas.

Ali sat back in the seat, nibbling on the hamburger, and had to stop herself from sighing. It tasted like ambrosia to her.

Sharp thought his luck had run out when he'd chased the signal for a hundred miles and come up behind a huge semi truck. They'd found the bug, and it had cost him hours of time to get back to 95 to leave the pictures at the motel. Then he'd gotten the call from the office that a motel manager had information.

He talked to the manager again, then headed north of the motel, guessing at what the cop was going to do. The most logical thing was to get rid of the Jeep. That meant stealing one, buying one or renting one. Stealing would be out. Buying was too complicated, and that left renting one. A rental was easier to come by and even easier to dump. He stopped by a phone booth, tore out the page in the phone book that advertised rental places in the area and got back into his car. As he kept driving north, he had Benny, one of Terrine's guys who was with him, call all the rental spots, one after the other, with the same story. He was calling for the police, looking for a kidnapper. Had anyone tried to rent a car with a cash deposit, instead of a credit card?

They hit pay dirt on the sixth call, and Benny handed Sharp the phone.

"Yeah, a guy called about renting this morning," the manager said. "And he wanted to take it on a cash deposit, instead of using a credit card."

"Did he ever show up?"

"You just missed him. He was here not more than fifteen minutes ago."

"Did he say where he was going?"

"Las Vegas, then Hoover Dam."

Sure, Sharp thought, and I'm the Easter Bunny. "Can I have a description of the car and the plate number?" The man hesitated, and Sharp added. "I can send one of my men there with a warrant to look at your books, if I have to."

"That's not necessary," the man said. "He took a '91 Chrysler Le Baron sedan, gray." Then he read off the license-plate number.

"Thanks," Sharp said, and hung up. "Where is that place?" he asked Benny.

The man picked up the torn page and read aloud, "Rent Rite Rentals in Marlow. That's east of here if you take the next turnoff. Do you think we can catch up with them?"

Sharp watched for the turnoff. "We'd better. If we don't, I wouldn't want to be Junior for anything."

"Hell, I wouldn't want to be us," Benny muttered.

Chapter 8

"How much farther do we have to drive?" Alicia asked, then sipped the last of her cola. The tepid liquid trickled down her throat while she watched Jack silently drive. The speedometer had hovered around seventy-five since they'd left Marlow, almost six hours ago.

"We'll stop in a while," he said, checking the rearview mirror, then the side mirrors. "I just hope we've left anyone following us in the dust."

"Excuse me," she said, and put her hand up.

He glanced at her, his blue eyes narrowed. "What?"

"You said if I don't understand something to ask. I don't understand exactly what we're doing. We keep driving, going farther and farther away from Las Vegas, but we have to be able to return there Monday morning."

He settled back in the seat, one hand resting loosely on the top of the steering wheel, the other gripping the wheel at the bottom. "It's called triangulation. Equal distances in three directions from the same location. You begin in Las Vegas and end there. We went northwest, now east, and tomorrow we'll hit a spot, then go southwest. We'll get back to the courthouse on time." He flashed her a smile, the best thing that had happened to her in a long time. "Trust me. It's my job."

She put her cup into the bag with the rest of the trash from lunch and sank back in the seat. She was beginning to trust him, and even though the security settled into her soul, there was still a basic fear of depending on anyone. Maybe she was more like Alicia than she thought. Her sister seldom trusted anyone. That's why she kept moving, never forming close relationships. Ali stayed at home doing basically the same thing. A day for revelations, she thought wryly, wondering why she hadn't realized that until this blue-eyed man walked into her life.

"Did you always want to be a blackjack dealer?" Jack asked, the question coming out of the blue.

Ali watched the desert baking under the afternoon sun, and she found herself telling Jack about herself, not about Alicia. "I wanted to be a photographer for as long as I can remember."

"Why?"

And another truth came from nowhere. "Maybe because a photographer can freeze life on film, and it can never be taken away, even after everything's long gone." And she knew she wanted to put Jack on film, to have something of the man after this fantasy was just a memory. Even if she had a cheap camera, she could capture that heartbeat of life. "No one can change it. No one."

"Why didn't you do something with that—" he asked, leaving unsaid the rest of the thought "—instead of becoming what you are?"

"I do. I mean, I did work for an ad agency."

"You didn't like that?"

"I loved it."

"But?" he prodded.

She hated lies, and she hedged. "Life changes. People change."

"Why would blackjack dealing be better than doing what you love?"

"It's what I want to do," she muttered.

"I guess a person like you does what she wants to do."

"You don't really know me," she blurted out.

Jack looked at her, then back at the road. "No, and I don't think Terrine, Jr. would know you looking like you do now."

"What do you mean?"

"No makeup or flashy clothes. You look almost wholesome." He laughed, but it was a humorless sound that raked across her nerves. "You know that Mick likes his women flashy and cheap."

"How do you know his taste in women?" she asked tightly.

"The man is about as secretive about that as he was when he was bragging to you about killing Milt Prince. If his men get to you and kill you, don't think he won't be bragging about that in the days to come."

She blanched and couldn't look at Jack. She stared out the side window, blindly watching the scenery whiz by. "Let's hope he won't be bragging," she murmured, and barely suppressed a shiver.

"Let's hope he won't be free."

She hugged herself. "I just don't understand why you have to...to even talk about it. I was the one who was shot at."

"As long as I'm with you, I'm in his way."

It hit her hard right then that Jack was putting his life on the line for a woman he didn't respect and probably wasn't even close to liking. "You could get killed."

"That's not in my plans."

She looked at Jack again, saw his jaw work and his hands tighten on the steering wheel. "Did you really almost kill Mick Terrine when you arrested him five years ago?"

His expression was grim. "Hell, yes. I told you, if Will hadn't pulled me off him, I'd be sitting in a cell now."

Despite the fact Jack was a cop, she had a hard time seeing him as a killer. "People get angry...."

"People don't have their hands around a person's neck, choking them, and people don't have to be pulled off them physically." He glanced at her, his eyes narrowed and unreadable, but she could see the tension in his shoulders and arms. "This time I'm letting the law take care of him. I don't want to see it screwed up in any way. So I let Will talk me into doing this, and I'm in it for the duration—no matter what."

He'd put up with anything, including a woman called Alicia Sullivan, to make sure Terrine didn't get off. "Is Will sure they can make the case stick this time?"

"Absolutely, as long as you arrive in one piece on Monday."

"I don't know much about cops or the law, except what I've seen on television or read in mysteries, but if Mick Terrine is so important to his father, a man you suggest is part of the mob, why doesn't Will offer Mick a deal to inform on his father's organization? Let him go into the Witness Protection Program, and let him change his name and location."

She didn't know what she expected, but it wasn't a burst of pure laughter. Jack shook his head, then ran a hand over his face as he sobered a bit. "I thought you knew Mick pretty well."

"I do, or at least, I thought so," she hedged.

"If you knew him very well at all, you'd know that being a Terrine is all Mick has going for him. If he informed and had to become Joe Blow, he'd be nothing. I think that terrifies him almost as much as life in prison. And if Mick ratted on his daddy, do you think big George would shrug his shoulders and let it go?"

"I don't know. He'd be mad, but—"

"Mad?" That brought more laughter. "That's rich. He'd have the kid taken out."

"Killed?"

"Without blinking."

"His own son?"

Jack sobered again. "Mick is George's son as long as he's got honor. If there isn't any honor, Mick is nothing. He'd be better off dead, as far as George would be concerned."

She sank back in her seat. A father would kill his own son? Killing her was one thing, but his own son? That chilled her to the core of her being. "He'd kill his son?"

"No, he'd have him killed." He shifted in his seat and took something out of his back pocket, then held it out to Ali. "This man, Sharp, does a lot of Terrine's dirty work. Did you ever see him around the kid?"

Ali took the photo, and at first she thought it was in black and white. Then she realized that the man, who was totally bald, wore a black suit, white shirt, had almost black eyes and stood against something white. He could have been anywhere from thirty to fifty, but she had never seen anyone look so cold, so removed. "I don't remember seeing him."

She went to hand the picture back to him, but he waved it off. "Put it in the glove compartment."

She did as he said, then sat back. "People can be so...so ugly, can't they?" she murmured.

"People can be just about anything."

"The Terrines hurt people, don't they?"

"Damn right they hurt people."

"How many stitches did you have in your chin and shoulder?" she heard herself ask.

Jack slowed the car and pulled to the side of the road. Ali looked around, but there was nothing here, just desert and shimmering heat that rose into a clear sky. "Why are we—"

Jack turned, his hand gripping the corner of her seat back. "A tire iron isn't a clean cut. I got ten stitches in my chin. Almost forty in my shoulder. Anything else you want to know?"

What she wanted was to reach out and touch the scar, to feel its irregularity under the tips of her fingers. She wanted to touch her lips to it, to taste— She cut off her thoughts and drew back. "I'm sorry. I just spoke without thinking."

"I bet you've done a lot of things without thinking," he muttered, then jammed the car in gear. In a cloud of dust and stones thrown by the tires, he took off onto the highway.

Ali gripped the sides of her seat and closed her eyes. No matter what she said or did, Jack judged her as if she was the person he thought Alicia was. It always came back to that, and there was nothing she could do about it.

Alicia sat by the hospital bed watching Lydia sleep. The elderly woman looked so frail and delicate, and Alicia had never thought of Lydia as old, just Lydia. She'd never doubted wherever she went, whatever she did, Lydia would always be there. She could always come home.

Suddenly that stability was in danger of being snatched away from her, the way it had been so often, early in her life. Alicia clenched her hands tightly in her lap and wished she had a cigarette, but she couldn't smoke in here.

She'd made a mess of so many things, always running, always looking for something she never found, something she couldn't even name. She watched Lydia breathe, short shallow breaths, then she stood and went to the window. She stared out over the city of Los Angeles to the blue blur of the Pacific far in the distance.

If she hadn't called Ali, she never would have known about Lydia's operation. That idea scared her most of all, even more than testifying against Mick. Lydia and Ali were all she had. Two people. Except for them, she had no one.

She closed her eyes. She hadn't told the police about Ali and Lydia, and if no one knew they were here, maybe she could come back here after the trial. Maybe she could melt into the millions of people in Los Angeles and still keep a semblance of her life.

She opened her eyes and pressed her hands palms down on the glass. She'd been running from her life for so long, and now she knew it was all she wanted. Her life.

"Ali?"

Alicia turned at the sound of her sister's name said in a weak whisper. She almost cried when she saw Lydia looking at her, the elderly woman's face touched with a slight smile.

"Oh, Lydia," she said, crossing to the bed to take her foster mother's hand. It felt cold, then the frail fingers closed around hers gently. "Thank God you woke up. I've been here for so long."

Lydia's faded blue eyes were faintly blurred from medication, but her free hand lifted and covered Alicia's holding hers. "You came," she whispered.

"Yes, I came." Alicia had to fight back tears. She might never have known about this at all. "I came."

The smile continued to flit at the corners of Lydia's mouth. "I knew you would, Alicia. I knew you'd come."

Alicia shouldn't have been surprised. She and Ali had never been able to fool Lydia when they were younger. "I always wondered—how can you tell us apart?"

"I just know." She glanced beyond Alicia, then back to her. "Where . . . where's Ali?"

Alicia sank down in the chair by the bed, still holding Lydia's hand. She knew there wasn't any reason to lie. Lydia could see through any fabrication in a minute. "She's in Las Vegas. She's doing something for me that I love her for."

Lydia frowned at Alicia. "Did you get her into trouble?"

"No. Not this time." She laughed, something she hadn't done in what seemed forever. "Ali's having a nice cozy weekend in a fancy hotel." She patted Lydia's hand. "Trust me, she's fine."

Ali looked up, and the setting sun was a rich backdrop for a town that spread out like a spider into the desert. A sign by the road proclaimed Everready, Nevada, pop. 8,000. Jack drove down the main drag, a street that was wide enough for two cars to pass with parking on the sides, but that was about it.

Everready was determinedly done in the Southwestern style, with whitewashed adobe buildings, plank sidewalks and Indian decorations on the shops that lined the way. Jack slowed, and Ali saw a two-story building, painted white with bright red trim, and shaped like an Indian adobe. A totem pole had been set into the front above the doors, beside a long sign that read Red Hawk Hotel.

Jack drove into a tiny parking lot to the left of the hotel, parked behind a van with the logo of the hotel on it, keeping out of sight from the street. He let the car idle. "Stay here while I go and register," he said. Unexpectedly he flicked the loose curls at her cheek. "Keep that hair out of sight."

His finger skimmed her cheek as he pulled his hand away and he jerked slightly as if the contact surprised him. Or maybe repulsed him. She didn't know anything anymore. Without another word, he turned from her and got out. In a moment he was out of sight, hidden by the van.

Ali knew a moment of complete isolation, a repeat of that moment when she'd watched his car pass her and drive away, and a repeat of something deep in her past. She hated it. She had to stop herself from getting out and going after him. She knew how foolish that would have been.

She thought she'd developed independence out of need, that she trusted few people and that she could get by on her own. How foolish she'd been to think that. The idea of Lydia's being gone almost killed her. Alicia had probably put herself in a position where she couldn't see her again, and all Jack had to do was be out of her sight and she panicked.

Ali made herself breathe in through her nose and out through her mouth, while she concentrated on staying calm. She would get through this and deal with the rest of her life when it faced her. She'd get through it. She would. By herself. She closed her eyes, pressed her hands palms down on her thighs and kept breathing in deeply through her nose and exhaling through her mouth.

The door clicked, and Ali jumped, then relaxed when she saw Jack open the driver's door and get in behind the wheel. "They have cottages behind the

main building. We'll be out of sight and relatively safe
for a while.''

He pushed the car into gear, swung back and drove
by the main building to the rear. On the left was a series of small buildings joined by breezeways for parking. They drove to the last one, parked the car in the
shade of the overhang, then got out.

Ali quickly circled the car and followed Jack up the
single step to the door of the whitewashed building.
Jack swung the door open, and Ali ducked past him
into the cool dimness of the cottage. In the gentle
shadows, Ali could make out two wood-framed beds
with soft turquoise spreads. The carpeting was a soft
rose that matched the curtains on two high windows
facing the hotel.

The place was old, but it had character and a sense
of belonging where it was. Belonging. Ali moved farther into the room while Jack closed the door. Had she
ever really belonged anywhere? She knew she came
closest with Lydia.

She turned to see Jack standing not more than two
feet from her, studying her intently. Instinctively she
knew that Jack belonged in his world in a way she'd
never known, and then the idea of her belonging to
him came without warning.

Tightness spread in her chest, and she turned away
from Jack. Belonging to him was just another fantasy that seemed bent on coming into her mind this
weekend. He didn't even know her real name. She
reached out and touched the post at the foot of the
closest bed. ''At least there are two beds this time.''

''No need for the Walls of Jericho tonight,'' Jack
said from behind her.

The innocent words, meant as a joke, made heat flood through her. She nodded and moved farther from Jack. She went to one of the windows at the front of the room and reached out to touch the softly woven mauve fabric of the curtain. But before she could, Jack was there. His hand covered hers and jerked it back.

"No," he said quickly. "Leave that closed. Don't you remember what happened last time you opened the drapes?"

She *did* remember, and she felt fear rise in her. Everything she'd tried not to think about rushed back at her, and she began to shake. She could have been killed, she thought, but then another thought came just as strongly, just as urgently.

Except for Alicia's involvement with Mick Terrine, she never would have known there was a Jackson Graham in this world. She never would have seen him, never have felt connected, never have thought he could protect her from every bad thing that ever happened or would happen.

The last thought made her light-headed, and she felt herself sway forward. The next thing she knew, she was in Jack's arms, being held so close to heat and strength that it all seemed a part of her. "I'm so scared," she whispered, and recognized that basic truth. But she couldn't tell him that the fear came as much from the fact he would walk out of her life on Monday as from the fact that the Terrines wanted her sister dead.

His arms surrounded her, his face buried in her hair, and she wished she could freeze time. She wished she could have this moment for the rest of her life, that she could hold on to him whenever she felt shaky or needful of connecting. But that seemed as foolish a wish as another one that came on the heels of that one. She wished Jack knew her, the *real* her, and that he liked what he saw, and that he wanted her to be with him.

The thought made her tremble. That would never happen. Never. She pressed her hands on his chest and reluctantly pushed back. But his hands never left her. They rested on her shoulders, and she dared to look up at him. All she saw was his eyes filled with a smoldering fire, one she could feel flickering to life in her, too. All she knew was the heat of his touch, his breath fanning her face, and all she wanted was to taste him again.

When his head lowered and his lips found hers, what had happened this morning faded into insignificance. Fire exploded in her, consuming her, and opening her mouth to Jack, inviting the pure pleasure of his kiss, seemed as natural as breathing. She circled his neck with her arms, arching toward him, feeling his strength against her breasts, his hips against hers. He wanted her, too. She could feel his desire growing against her, and it only added to the fires that flamed out of control.

Ali had never wanted a man like this before. She'd never felt an impulse to know another human being so completely and wonderfully. His tongue skimmed her teeth, invading her, tasting her, and she willingly gave herself up to the sensations. To know Jack was the one thing she wanted, to know him and to have him, and to lose herself completely. She moaned softly as his hands trailed down her back to her hips and pulled her tightly against him.

Jack had known fear in his life, over and over again on his job, when he'd faced the wrong side of a gun or had known that in a heartbeat he could be dead. But he had never known this fear he felt holding Ali in his arms. And this fear was total and encompassing. It plunged deep into his being, into his soul. He wanted this woman with a single-mindedness that took his breath away. He wanted her next to him, skin against skin, heat mingling with heat. He wanted her in his bed, coming to him in the shadows, her essence filling him and completing him.

He held her against him, almost willing her to blend with him, to become one with him, as if he could inhale her and know her. His desire was raw and white-hot, his need so overwhelming he was shaking from it. And it scared him, it scared the hell out of him. He moved with Ali back toward the bed and fell down on the soft spread with her.

The feeling of her under him only inflamed him more. The rise of her breasts against his chest stunned him. And he wanted her in a way he had never wanted any woman before. He loved her mixture of vulnerability and sensuality, and when his hand found her breast, felt its fullness straining against the thin cotton cover, he heard her moan. The soft shuddering sound seemed to surround him and invade him all at once.

He felt her nipple peak under the soft fabric, then he only wanted to feel her skin, to know her without any barriers, and his hand tugged at the cotton. At the same moment that he felt her swelling breast under his hand, the peaking of her nipple, he knew exactly what he wanted. He wanted to know her the way no man ever could, or ever had.

As that thought settled into his soul, his hand stilled on her. No man. He felt a chill suffocating the heat. No man except Mick Terrine. Cold water couldn't have sobered him more surely than that singular thought. Mick Terrine. He was following in the footsteps of Mick Terrine. The insanity of desire fled, and Jack pulled back.

Even though he tried to avoid looking at Ali, he had a flashing glimpse of her before he turned away. Her hair was a riot of color and curls around her flushed face. Her lips were parted, her eyes heavy with desire and her shirt tugged high, revealing perfect breasts with rosy peaks. His whole body tightened horribly, making it awkward for him to roll off the bed and stand with his back to her.

He stood very still, so angry with himself that he wished he could scream to the heavens. And that anger only grew when he finally turned and saw Ali. She was tugging at her shirt, trying to sit up, then she pushed her hair back from her face and her eyes met his. All he had to do was look at her and he wanted her. The evidence of that desire was hard to hide, but he tried to ignore it and gather his thoughts.

Ali stared up at Jack, not daring to lower her eyes below his chest. Shock was robbing her of the ability to speak. She'd come so close to giving herself to him, to losing herself in the moment, that it made her physically sick. That sickness only increased when she looked into his eyes and saw a burning anger that stunned her. Her breasts still tingled from his touch, and something deep in her, something she didn't understand, something she couldn't even name, throbbed and ached.

She closed her eyes to shut out the sight of the man in front of her, and she had to try twice before she could speak. "What are we going to do now?" she asked.

Jack was silent for a moment, then spoke, but his answer had nothing to do with what had just happened between them. "I think I should contact Will and tell him what's been going on. You stay here. I'll be back as soon as I get through."

She heard Jack move across the floor, then the door open and close. Silence was all around her. She got off the bed and quickly crossed the room to lock the door. She leaned back against the cool wood and wrapped her arms tightly around herself, as if she could hold herself together by her own determination. One part of her needed Jack with her, yet the other part, the sane part, didn't even know what she'd do when he came back.

When Jack left, Ali felt an intense loneliness that she tried to convince herself was because Jack was the only person standing between her and Mick Terrine. But she couldn't. She more than depended on Jack. She felt connected to him in some intangible way, even though they'd only met a day ago. And she knew it would be very easy for her to fall in love with him.

That thought stopped her dead. Love? She shook her head. No. Not love. Especially not under circumstances where he thought she was Alicia. Maybe if she could get through this, if Alicia came back on Monday and everything worked out, she could explain things to him. Maybe he'd understand. And maybe he'd understand that she had no choice, that she had to do what she did. Or maybe he'd never understand her breaking the law, or how she could risk everything for her sister and foster mother.

The sound of a car engine outside jerked her out of her thoughts, and she listened. A door closed softly, then she could hear movement on the gravel parking area. Someone checking in, she thought, but as the sound of murmured voices filtered into the room, she crossed to the window. Carefully she touched the drapery fabric and nudged it aside a fraction of an inch. She looked out and saw a dark car parked crossways behind the Le Baron, blocking it from backing up, and two men near it.

A dark heavyset man stood by the Le Baron, and another man, completely bald, was moving around the car, peering in the windows at the sides and back. She knew who he was. Sharp. The man in the photo that Jack had shown her. She looked beyond the cars, but couldn't see anyone.

Jack would be coming back any minute, and he'd walk right into them. Fear for him choked her, and she had to concentrate on breathing, in through her nose, out through her mouth, and remarkably, her thoughts began to clear.

Maybe Jack had already spotted them. He could have when they pulled in. All she knew was she couldn't stay here. She dropped the curtain back into

place, then quickly pushed a chair under the door-
knob.

With her heart hammering in her ears, she franti-
cally looked around for another way out, but there
were no other doors, just windows. She grabbed her
purse, then went into the bathroom and locked the
door. The window in there was high, but wide enough
for her to get through. If she stood on the tub, she
could unlatch the hinged window, push it up, then step
on the faucet and lever herself up.

She stretched to open the window, then she tossed
her purse out and heard it land with a soft thud on the
ground below. Quickly she climbed up, one foot on the
faucet, and she gripped the sill with both hands. Pulling herself up, she managed to get her head through
the window, which looked out onto a storage area. She
tugged her leg up, got her knee on the sill, then she
maneuvered herself up and out through the window.

She slid down the wall, then let go of the sill and
landed on the dirt right by her purse. She heard a
knock from the front of the cottage, and she quickly
scooped up her purse. Keeping close to the wall, she
edged her way along the adobe until she got to the
corner. She looked around the side of the building,
saw it was clear, then ran across the opening to the
back of the next cottage.

She made her way to the back of the main building
and then circled it on the far side. Then she went into
a dirt alley that ran up to the street. She hurried along
it, praying that Jack was still at the pay phone. She
reached the street. Cautiously she peeked around the

side and saw that the front porch of the hotel was empty. She listened and couldn't hear anyone coming. Bracing herself, she stepped out of the alley and headed for the hotel entrance.

Chapter 9

Just as Ali reached for the wooden door, it swung open and Jack was there. He saw her, his eyes widening, then he came toward her as the door swung shut behind him. In one fluid movement, he had her by the arm, looked up and down the street, then pulled her along the porch to the alleyway.

With his body shielding her from the street, he all but pinned her against the rough adobe of the hotel wall. He was so close she could see his nostrils flare with each breath and feel the racing beat of his heart against her breasts. "What in the hell are you trying to do?" he demanded in a harsh whisper.

"They . . . they found us," she managed. "Sharp—that bald man—he's here."

"What?"

"Out . . . outside the cottage. He was looking at the car with another man."

"Who?"

"He's dark, heavy."

"Benny."

She touched her tongue to her cold lips. "How could they find us?"

He closed his eyes tightly for a moment, then opened them. "Damned if I know. What are they driving?"

"A big car, dark, sort of like a limousine, but not quite that long, and it's parked behind our car, blocking it."

"Damn," Jack muttered, then moved away from her and went to the corner of the building. He looked in both directions, then came back to Ali. "We have to move and do it now."

"But the car—"

"—is yesterday's news. We're out of here." He grabbed her hand and said, "We'll go back the way we came. There's a truck stop that way, a restaurant, phones. Maybe we can figure out what to do by the time we get there."

As they stepped out onto the sidewalk, Ali had such a sense of being exposed that she instinctively moved closer to Jack. Without breaking stride, he slipped his hand out of hers and casually slipped his arm around her shoulders, pulling her against his side as they walked.

The contact gave her the strength to move with him, to keep going down the street and not turn to look back. "They'll follow us, won't they?" she asked.

"They'll try. It's up to us to make sure they don't, or that we get a good head start on them."

She liked the feeling of his voice vibrating against her side as he spoke, and she slipped her arm around his waist. It really was the two of them in this together, and that thought gave her some strength. "How can we do that?"

"I don't have any idea." His hold on her tightened as they kept walking. "We'll have to figure it out as we go."

When they approached the truck stop, a series of buildings clustered in the blanketing heat of dusk, Jack guided Ali toward the restaurant that sat under a huge red-and-yellow flashing neon sign. "We need distance between us and them," he said close to her ear. "The sooner the better."

He kept walking with her, heading for the gas pumps that sat at the far side of the restaurant in front of a metal Quonset-hut garage. An old pickup truck was idling by the nearest set of pumps, and Jack shifted to take Ali's hand as he approached the truck. Ali saw the driver, an older man with craggy features and leathery skin set off by a full mustache.

"Sir," Jack said, and the man turned to him, his eyes narrowed.

"What do you need?" the man asked in a gravelly voice.

"Our rental car broke down back there, and they can't fix it until tomorrow. We really could use a lift to the next town."

"I ain't going that far, but I could take you to the intersection for the highway."

Jack agreed quickly. "That'd be great."

"Climb in. I'm ready to go."

Jack and Ali hurried around the front of the truck and got into the cab. It smelled of age, a bit of beer and a lot of animals. Ali shifted on the hard seat, staying close to Jack, and she was grateful when he put his arm along the back of the seat and let his hand rest on her shoulder.

The driver pushed the truck into gear. It shook, then took off slowly out onto the road and back through town. "Name's Crane," the elderly man said as he glanced at Ali and Jack. "Conrad Crane, but everyone calls me Crane."

"We're Mary and Paul Jeffers," Jack said easily.

Crane nodded. "You two in trouble?"

Jack's hand on Ali jerked slightly, but when he spoke, he bluffed. "Having the car break down could be called trouble."

"No, ain't that. There's something else. But you don't have to tell me. I can mind my own business."

"Thanks," Jack said.

Sharp didn't believe in luck. Never had. But when he spotted the gray sedan the rental company had told him about parked off the street, it was pure luck. If he hadn't slowed, if he hadn't looked right then, he would have been past and never known he'd passed it by. But he *had* looked, and the Le Baron had been just visible from the road.

He stared at it, then at the cottage it was parked in front of. Too easy, he thought, but didn't question the fates. He just wanted to finish the job and get the hell back to the city. He motioned to Benny that he was going in, then he moved quietly to the door of the cottage. His gun out, he rapped on the wooden barrier with his knuckles.

Nothing. He knocked again. "Room service," he called out.

When there was no response, he pressed his ear to the door. There wasn't a sound inside. He turned to Benny and motioned for him to go around back of the cottage and keep it covered. He waited until Benny was out of sight, then he tried the knob. It was locked. He glanced left and right, couldn't see anyone, then reached into his pocket and took out a pick. He jimmied the lock, heard it click, then pushed. It didn't give.

He glanced around again, then stood back, raised his foot and kicked the door as hard as he could. He heard a crack and the sound of splintering wood, then the door swung back. A quick look inside showed a broken chair and empty rooms. He came back out, called to Benny, then hurried to the main office of the hotel.

Ten minutes later after the clerk had told them Mr. and Mrs. Jeffers had walked off down the street, Sharp and Benny were at the gas pumps talking to the station owner. "Sure, I seen her," the short man in greasy clothes said as he examined Alicia's picture. "She and some guy just got in a truck and took off."

"What truck?" Sharp asked.

"Old man Crane's truck. He gave them a ride out toward his place."

"Where's his place?"

"You can't miss it. He's the first ranch after the intersection for the main highway."

The man gave the picture back to Sharp. "Is something wrong?"

"Yeah, the woman was kidnapped," Sharp said.

The man frowned. "She didn't look like she was in any danger."

Sharp shook his head and motioned for Benny to bring the car up. "Some people just don't know how close they are to real danger."

Crane slowed the truck at the intersection, but as Jack was about to get out, the old man stopped him. "Listen, son, I can tell you two've got a problem. I'm not interfering, but do you think it's best to be out here trying to hitchhike? You'll have a devil of a time getting a ride this late."

"That's all right," Jack said, the idea of trusting anyone right now unthinkable. "We'll manage. Thanks for your help."

"I'm telling you, you'll be here all night." Crane glanced at the sky where the light was fading quickly. "I'm not prying, but I don't think this is the place to be."

Jack knew the man was right. They couldn't just stand by the side of the road with their thumbs out. They'd probably have to find a safe spot and camp. He felt Ali shift by his side, sensing her uneasiness, and he tightened his hand on her shoulder. She stilled, not looking at him, but he knew she was thinking the same thing he was. Why was a stranger being so concerned about them? Did the Terrine web of power reach down to a weathered old guy in a beat-up truck?

Jack decided there was nothing to lose by being direct. "Why are you concerned?"

The old guy looked Jack right in the eye. "I told you. I can tell when someone's in trouble. But I'm not asking what. I'm just saying that I'm willing to help. If you need help."

Jack made a decision in that moment. Right or wrong, he'd take this as far as he could. "All right, what alternatives do you have to us thumbing it?"

"Well, it ain't much, but I got an extra room. You're welcome to it for the night. It ain't the Ritz, but it'll be comfortable—and keep you out of sight."

"Where's your place?"

"Five miles straight ahead."

"Before I let you do this, you'd better know that there could be a problem."

"Had problems all my life," Crane said. "I can handle them. Lots of practice."

Jack hesitated, feeling Ali tensing beside him. "We'd appreciate it, Mr. Crane."

"Just call me Crane." The old pickup backfired, then took off from the intersection.

Jack looked around Ali to speak to the old man. "I'll try to keep you out of this."

"I can take care of myself, Mr. Jeffers," Crane said.

Jack instinctively trusted this man, and he just hoped his instincts were working. "My name's Jack, and this is Ali. There are two men looking for us, and they aren't looking to give us medals."

"The cops?"

"No." Jack shifted and took out his badge. He flipped the cover open and held it out to Crane. "That's me." Crane glanced at it, then nodded. "Thought so. Knew you weren't bad." He drove onto a side road, then slowed at a cattle gate to the left. He swung through the open gate and drove down a lane lined with the shadows of huge trees. In a few minutes, they broke into a clearing.

Ali trusted Jack, and it was plain to see he'd made a decision to trust Crane. So would she. She looked ahead at a rambling farmhouse with fencing on either side, and flat land stretching out into the coming night.

Crane stopped the truck by the house and the three of them got out. The old man led the way to a wraparound porch, and he pulled open a screen door to let them into his house.

Ali stepped into what, in days gone by, would have been called a parlor—a cluttered room with overstuffed furniture, busy wall paper, scatter rugs and a tulip-shade fixture overhead. It smelled of age, maybe pipes and animals. Then she saw two huge dogs, lying in front of the couch, raise their heads to look at them. Their muzzles were gray, and they looked like a cross between Great Danes and small horses.

"Caesar and Cleo aren't the best watchdogs, but they look imposing," Crane said as he let the screen door close with a snap. In unison, the dogs settled back with a sigh and went on sleeping.

"This way," Crane said, and moved to his left. Circling the furniture, he went into a short hall, with Ali and Jack following. He stopped by one of two closed doors and pushed it back. "This is the guest suite," he said with a smile, and stood aside.

Ali looked past the two men into a room the size of a walk-in closet, a walk-in closet almost filled by a single bed. Sleeping in that bed with Jack was out of the question. After everything, she couldn't take that now. As if Jack had read her mind, he stood back to let her pass. "Why don't you get ready for bed? I need to talk to Mr. Crane for a while."

Ali didn't know what to say, so she silently went past the two men into the small room. "The bathroom's right across the hall," Crane said. "Sleep well. I won't keep your man too long."

Ali nodded, and as the door shut, she stood in the middle of the tiny room. One bed. Not even a chair. She didn't know what she was going to do. No Walls of Jericho would work here. But she was so tired. For now she'd just rest, and when Jack came in, she'd figure out what to do. She climbed onto the bed, on top of the faded quilted spread and curled up in a ball on her side.

Jack went back into the living room with Mr. Crane and sank into one of two worn easy chairs positioned to face the television and had a clear view of the front door. Crane looked at Jack. "How about a drink? You look like you could use one."

"That sounds good," Jack said.

As the old man went to a breakfront along the side wall and poured whiskey into two glasses, he said, "Have a drink, then we'll talk."

Jack couldn't tell the man he just had wanted to get out of the bedroom. Any excuse would have done. He listened but couldn't hear any sound coming from the bedroom, and he relaxed a bit. There was no way he was going back into that room tonight. Ali could have the bed all to herself. He'd stay out here and sleep in this chair if he had to. He accepted the drink from

Crane, took a sip of the burning liquid, then sat back with a sigh.

Before he could take another drink lights flashed outside and then there was the sound of a car coming closer. Crane looked out the door, then back at Jack who sat bolt upright. "Dark car coming up slow. This who you expected?"

"It's sooner than I expected, but chances are it's them."

"Well, we'll just see what they want. You get out of sight."

Jack got up, glass in hand, and moved quickly into the hallway. The dogs lifted their heads briefly, then settled back to sleep. "Great watchdogs," Jack muttered as he pressed himself against the wall and looked around the corner so he could see the front door. Crane stepped outside, and Jack heard a car stop. Two doors opened and closed, then a voice Jack knew belonged to Sharp asked, "Are you Mr. Crane?"

"Yes, sir, and who'd you be?"

"I'm with the police. We're looking for a kidnap victim." His voice came closer as he spoke. "This is a picture of her."

There was silence, then Crane asked, "She was kidnapped?"

"Yes. We were told that you picked up a couple back in town. Sounded like the ones we're looking for."

Jack tensed as Crane said, "Sure did. Pretty little thing with bright red hair. Got a temper, I bet. The guy with her, he said he was her husband and they were honeymooners."

"Where'd you take them?" Sharp asked.

"I dropped them at the intersection about five miles back. You might have passed them if you came that way. They were going to hitch a ride. Saw a semi stop as I was driving off. He might have given them a ride."

"Did you see any markings on the truck?"

"No, sir, didn't see a one. Just seen the truck. Big, with a black cab."

"What did the trailer look like?"

"Double. Gray, I think. Wish I could tell you more."

Jack heard footsteps, then Crane's voice again, farther away and muffled. "Kidnapped, you say?" The next thing Jack could hear clearly was the closing of car doors and an engine starting up. The car drove away, then the sound of footsteps on the porch. The front door opened and closed, and Crane said, "They're gone."

Jack came out and faced Crane across the room. "I suppose I should explain a bit more to you."

"I'd sure be interested in what you've got to say."

"I'll explain everything, but first I want to check on Ali."

"I'll be right here," Crane said, crossing to the breakfront.

Jack went down the hall. He opened the door to the bedroom, found the side light on, then he crossed to the bed. Ali was sound asleep, lying on her side, her knees drawn up to her stomach. The soft light touched the hollow at her cheek and cast shadows where her long lashes lay in fans against her skin.

He clutched his half-finished drink, then raised the glass and downed the alcohol in one swallow. As the liquid burned down his throat, he studied Ali in sleep.

It was a peculiar form of torture to watch her like this, a self-imposed torture, as if he could wipe out his need to touch her just by forcing himself to see her like this.

But nothing seemed to kill that need in him to touch her, to explore her, to know her. And he knew with a numbing certainty that no matter who she'd been with, who had touched her and held her and made love to her, she touched him on levels he'd never before experienced.

But she wouldn't again. He wouldn't let her.

He turned from the sight and slipped out of the room, closing the door. He went back into the living room and crossed to the chair. Sinking into it, he held his empty glass out to Crane, who was still by the breakfront. "I could use another." Maybe a drink or two would blot out the images bombarding his mind. The way the delicate curls lay against Ali's temple, the soft flutter of the pulse at the hollow of her throat, her slender hands folded like a child's and tucked under her cheek.

"More whiskey?" Crane asked.

"My first choice," Jack murmured, trying to still his thoughts.

"Mine, too," Crane muttered as he reached for the bottle and crossed to Jack. "Mine, too."

When Ali awoke in the morning she was clutching a pillow to her chest and sunlight was slanting into the room through a small parting in the curtains. As she rolled onto her back, it took her a minute to realize where she was, then she reached to her right. The bed was empty. Twisting to look, she could tell that she had slept alone all night.

She lay very still. She couldn't hear anything, and she had a horrible feeling that no one was here. Just her. She got up, found the clip she'd worn in her hair lying on the floor, and she grabbed it, then pushed it into her pocket. Smoothing her top, she went to the door.

She stepped out into the hall and hurried to the living room. As she got to the doorway, she stopped. The dogs looked as if they hadn't moved all night, still sleeping, still side by side in front of the couch. Then her heart rose in her throat.

She saw Jack sprawled in one easy chair, Crane in the other, his head lolling to one side. For a heartbeat Ali thought the two men were dead, and the world seemed to freeze around her. Then she inhaled and knew how wrong she'd been.

The smell of whiskey drifted in the air, and as she went closer to Jack, she saw a glass lying on its side on the carpet by his chair just inches from his slack fingers. An empty bottle of whiskey lay at Crane's feet, along with another glass. They weren't dead. They'd passed out, drunk.

She moved closer and heard a low snoring sound coming from Crane. Then she moved to Jack and stood over him. She stifled an urge to reach out and brush errant strands of hair off his forehead. To touch the scar at his chin. The need to make physical contact with this man was like a hunger in her. She literally had to clench her hands at her sides to keep from touching him. *There are no anchors in this world,* she told herself. *No anchors. Not even this man.*

"Jack?" she said.

He didn't move. Ali bent closer and stopped breathing when she inhaled a mingling of male essence, traces of after-shave and the mellow odor of whiskey. Tentatively she poked at Jack's shoulder and he stirred, then settled again with a sigh. Ali crouched down by the chair. "Jack," she said, "wake up," and she poked his arm again.

Jack had been hung over before, but he had never felt a throbbing quite like this in his head as sleep was stripped away from him. For a moment he couldn't remember why he'd sat up half the night drinking the cheap whiskey, then as he stirred and opened his eyes into slits, he knew.

His gaze slowly focused on Ali standing beside him, her hair in wild disarray, her clothes mussed, yet her beauty struck him to his soul. The whiskey had been the only alternative to going into her bed last night. And he wouldn't have been responsible for what might have happened if he'd been that close to her in the dark.

His stomach clenched at the images that flitted into his mind, and he swallowed hard to control the rising sourness from the remnants of the whiskey. She had no right to look so appealing, and he had no right even to think what he was thinking. He sat forward and buried his head in his hands.

"Did you sleep out here all night?" Ali asked, her voice touched with husky amusement.

I had no choice, he wanted to say, but settled for a simple, "I guess so." He ran his tongue over his lips and around the cottony dryness in his mouth. "What time is it?"

"Just after seven."

Jack had almost forgotten about Crane until the man spoke up, his voice annoyingly clear and sober-sounding. "Do you think those guys'll come by again?"

"Those guys?" Ali asked, and he felt her move. She crouched in front of him, her hands on his knees, her fingers pressing against the denim of his jeans. He jerked at the contact and muttered a low oath when his head felt as if it would either explode or fall off.

Carefully he raised his head and found himself looking into her green eyes. *Please, don't look at me with that fear and trust, as if I have all the answers,* he thought. Then he deliberately grabbed both arms of the chair to keep from touching her and drawing her close.

Crane was moving around the room, the man obviously a lot more resistant to bad whiskey than Jack was. "Coffee, anyone?" he asked. "Or do you want the hair of the dog that bit you, Jack?"

"Coffee," Jack said without looking at him. He couldn't take his eyes off Ali crouched in front of him. "They were here last night after you went to bed. Sharp and Benny. They left, and I don't think they'll be back this way. They'll be looking for a semi."

"How do they keep finding us?" she asked, her lips not at all steady. She stood and moved away from him.

Jack grimaced as he raked his fingers through his hair and sat back. "Damned if I know." Carefully he got out of the chair, being sure not to jar his head. "We should get going."

Crane came back into the room and put three mugs of steaming coffee on the table by the chairs. "If you got a few minutes, I could whip up some eggs and bacon, or maybe pancakes?''

Jack felt his stomach lurch at just the mention of food. "Thanks, but I'll pass." He picked up the coffee mug and looked at the old man who seemed completely free of any hangover. "Just point me to the bathroom."

"The door across from the bedroom. Plenty of hot water."

"Thanks," Jack mumbled, and walked slowly out of the room.

"There's some clean shirts in the cupboard in the bathroom. Help yourself, Jack."

"Thanks," Jack said again, and kept going until he got to the bathroom. He went into the small room, closed the door and crossed to the pedestal sink. He put his coffee mug on the side, then gripped the porcelain with both hands. Slowly he raised his head to look in the mirror. Meeting the gaze of his bloodshot eyes, he knew he looked just the way he felt—like a long mile of bad road.

He turned on the cold water, cupped it in his hands and splashed his face. He did that over and over until he felt his head beginning to clear. Finally he stopped, gripped the sink again and stood very still. He'd been stupid to drink like that, trying to hide from his reactions to Ali in cheap whiskey. "Dumb stupid thing to do," he muttered at his reflection. But that didn't stop him from remembering the sight of her sleeping, or that look of fear in her eyes moments ago.

He picked up his coffee, took a deep gulp of the strong brew, and in that moment he knew he'd do anything to keep Ali safe. Anything.

After a shower and the loan of a clean shirt, Jack felt almost human. As he stepped into the living room about ten minutes later, he smelled toast and coffee in the air. Ali was in the chair he'd slept in, sitting across from Crane, her legs curled up under her and a plate on her lap. She popped her last piece of toast into her mouth, then looked up at him. "Feel better?" she asked, a hint of a smile in her voice.

"Better than what?" he muttered.

She let that go. "Do you want some eggs and toast?" She stood with the empty plate in her hand. "It wouldn't take a minute, and I—"

"Thanks, but no thanks. Why don't you freshen up and we'll be on our way." He crossed to the screen door and looked out. The driveway was empty and there was no sound other than the hum of insects in the already hot air. They had to leave. Sharp was no fool, and sooner or later he'd know he'd been had by Crane.

He heard Ali move, and when he knew she'd gone into the bathroom and the door had closed, he turned to Crane, who was still in his chair. "I don't know how to thank you for doing all this."

"Don't thank me, boy. It's the most excitement I've had in a year of Sundays."

Jack started to smile, but the effort was almost painful. "Let's hope it's the last of that excitement."

"How am I going to know if you two are okay after you leave here?"

"Just watch the news. You'll see something in a few days."

He frowned at Jack. "It's that big?"

"I'm afraid so." Jack raked his fingers through his damp hair, not totally remembering what he'd told Crane last night while they drank. "It'll be settled soon, and hopefully we'll all be in one piece."

"You take care of that pretty little thing, won't you?"

"That's my job," Jack said, and knew the magnitude of that lie.

"I got an idea," Crane said as he stood.

"What's that?"

"You need transportation. You can take my truck."

Jack started to shake his head, but stopped when the motion only added to his physical pain. "I appreciate it, but those guys know what it looks like, and they're probably still out there searching for us."

Crane nodded, and Jack envied him the ability to move his head without obvious discomfort. "Yeah, I guess so. What do you want to do?"

Jack spotted the phone on the wall by the kitchen door. "Can I use your phone?"

"Sure."

Jack dialed direct to Will's house. As soon as he heard Will on the other end, he quickly told him what had happened. There was a low vibrating oath, then Will said, "Find a safe place, and I'll send someone for you."

"No, I'll get us in. Just be ready for trouble."

"All right. Do what you think is best."

"What about Terrine's inside contact?"

"I've got my ideas, and I've dropped a few red herrings to find out for sure."

"Anyone I know?"

"Looks that way. If my plan works, he'll be out of your way within the next few hours."

Jack sensed that Ali was back. The air wafted with freshness of soap and water and whatever it was that made her Ali. He turned, and although he'd braced himself, he still felt the impact of the sight of her standing by the hall door. Her hair was loose, with damp curls clinging to her face, which was slightly flushed from the shower. She wore a T-shirt of Crane's and she was carrying her shoes.

Her eyes met his, then quickly looked away to Crane. Turning his back on her, Jack said into the phone, "Those red herrings?"

"Yeah?"

"Draw them away from the southeast route. All right?"

"Done."

"Catch us when we fall," he murmured, then hung up. He took a five-dollar bill out of his pocket, laid it on top of the phone for the call, then turned and saw Ali and Crane talking by the front door.

As Jack crossed to them, Crane asked, "Got it settled?"

"I guess so. If you could take us to the highway, we'll get out of here and leave you in peace."

"Hate to do that. What if they're still hanging around?"

"With any luck, they'll be going in the other direction." He looked at Ali. "Are you ready to get going?"

She smiled, a slow gentle expression that made the throbbing in his head intensify. "Are you in any condition to leave?"

"I'll live," he murmured, hoping he was telling the truth.

Chapter 10

Crane stopped the truck at the on ramp for the main highway and kept the engine idling. He squinted at Jack and Ali. "You two be safe, hear?"

Ali hated to get out of the truck, but she knew there weren't any options. They had to move on. Jack opened the door and climbed down, then held out his hand to Ali. She grabbed her purse and accepted Jack's help as she got out of the truck, then his support was gone.

Jack looked back into the cab. "Thanks for everything. I'll be in touch when this is all over and done."

"You do that." Crane smiled at Ali. "Hope it all works out for you."

She wondered if anything would work out for her, but she smiled back at him. "You've certainly helped two strangers."

"Ain't no such thing as a stranger, just someone you haven't met yet," he said.

Ali glanced at Jack. That was the way she felt about him. He'd never been a stranger, just someone she'd been waiting to meet, and it seemed as if she'd been waiting all her life. She hooked the strap of her purse on her shoulder. "I'll send back your shirt."

Crane laughed. "Keep it. It looks better on you than it ever did on me."

"You'll be hearing from me," Jack said.

"Make sure I do." Crane revved the engine. "Take care, you two."

Jack swung the door shut and stood by Ali as Crane's truck lurched forward, then drove off. He looked around, then led the way to the entrance to the highway and to a small tree near the edge of the pavement.

"What do we do now?" Ali asked as she followed him, her purse heavy with the bottle of water and cookies Crane had insisted they take with them.

"Wait."

She plopped the purse on the ground in the shade, then looked at Jack. "Then what?"

"We get as close as we can to Las Vegas, then wait until morning. We have to be at the courthouse between eight-thirty and nine." He sank down onto the parched ground under the tree. "Hopefully someone will come by and give us a ride."

Ali sat by him, hugging her knees and staring out at the oppressively hot day. "And what if we're sitting here when Sharp and his friend come back to look for us?"

"I've thought about that," he said. "With any luck, they're going back the way we came."

"Why would they?"

"Will thinks he knows who their contact is. He didn't name names, but he's dropping a hint that we're coming in from the northwest, the way we left."

"And if that person isn't their contact?"

"Boy, you're starting to think like a cop. Never take anything for granted. Never believe that things will go the way you planned them."

"That comes from being human," she admitted. Things certainly hadn't gone the way she'd planned ever since she'd gotten the phone call from Alicia.

"Yeah, and cops are human."

She knew that Jack Graham was human, and very much male. She shifted a bit away from him on the dusty ground, under the pretense of looking for something in her purse. She'd all but forgotten the purse was actually Alicia's, and when she found a pair of glasses, she pulled them out. "Sunglasses," she murmured, and slipped them on.

The oversize lenses offered much-needed protection from the glare. "Boy, these are great," she said.

He stared at her, his mouth thinned, then he turned from her and looked down the road. "You act as if you're surprised they're in there."

She caught herself and covered with a quick lie. "I...I thought I'd lost them." She pushed them higher on her nose. "I just wish I'd found them before."

Jack stood and moved the few feet to the edge of the pavement. "If I spot anyone that looks suspicious, take off for that gully about twenty feet back. Get in, keep your head down and—"

"—and don't ask questions," she said to his back.

"You've got it down pat," he said tightly.

Ali stared at Jack, at his rigid stance and the tightness in his shoulders. "I'm a fast learner," she murmured.

Silence fell between them, and all that could be heard was the occasional vehicle and the high-pitched humming of insects. Ali moved back, weary of Jack cutting her off the way he did. She rested her head against the rough trunk of the tree and knew she *was* a fast learner. In a matter of days, she'd learned that the person she had been for twenty-seven years was waiting for something to happen.

Now it had, and it had come in the form of blinding lightning, destroying everything in its wake. She looked away from Jack. If Lydia survived, if Alicia survived, if she survived, maybe she could make some sense of her life. Although a life without Jack wouldn't make any sense at all. She closed her eyes. One more lesson she'd learned.

For more than half an hour, no one stopped. Cars sped up and passed them by, and trucks never hesitated to keep going. Ali had watched the ramp most of the time, until the land began to blur and shimmer. The baking heat was oppressive, and it was making the T-shirt stick to her skin. "I feel so exposed out here," she said finally, as she stood and tugged the cotton away from her skin.

Jack looked at her, the heat causing a thin film of moisture on his skin. "So do I, but there aren't any options."

Ali heard the heavy throbbing of a truck engine, then Jack held out his hand, thumb up. A diesel truck with a high-sided flatbed trailer was coming up the ramp, and she fully expected it to keep going. But amazingly it slowed and the brakes ground as it stopped in front of them.

The fumes from the diesel filled the air along with an odor she could only describe as wet socks mixed with manure. It made her grimace, then she saw the reason for the smell. Through the narrow gaps in the stakes of the truck bed, she could see a small herd of sheep.

Jack pulled himself up to the passenger door by grabbing a rail on the side of the cab, then he tugged the door open. Ali couldn't hear the conversation, but Jack finally jumped down and looked at her. "We can't ride in the cab. It's against company policy, but we can sit in a jump seat in the back."

"With those?" she asked incredulously, pointing to the bleating sheep.

"It looks like it's that, or we can keep waiting for a ride. Personally I vote for this." Jack moved to the side of the trailer and tugged on a handle near the back. A wooden slat door opened, and he motioned Ali to get in.

She inched toward the open door until she could see inside. Instead of the expected sheep, there was a bench in a narrow section, partitioned from the main cargo by heavy wire. Sheep were pressed against the wire. "You're kidding, aren't you?"

"It's this, or we sit out here in the heat waiting. Your call."

She looked at Jack, at the sheen of perspiration, the shirt clinging damply to his chest and shoulders, and she knew she looked just as hot and tired. "All right," she murmured, and gripped the door with one hand.

With Jack's help, she levered herself into the small section against the cab. The smell was incredible, the heat oppressive, and the noise of bleating sheep was everywhere. She sank onto the hard bench while Jack got in, then closed the door. As he sat down next to her, he knocked on the back of the cab and the truck took off.

Ali moved close enough to Jack to be heard over the racket of the sheep. "How far can he take us?"

"He said he'd let us off in Bixby. It's about a hundred miles outside Vegas and close enough for us to make it there in the morning." Unexpectedly she felt his hand cover hers on her thigh, and she turned her hand upward to lace her fingers with his. "It's almost over," he said, his voice a low rumble near her ear.

"Thank goodness," she said. "I don't know how much more I can take."

Jack moved even closer to her. "You're doing fine. You spotted Terrine's men and saved our skins. Now all we have to do is make it to the courthouse."

"That's all," she echoed, her voice shaky at best.

"We'll do it," he said, his hold on her hand tightening.

Without thinking about rhyme or reason, she leaned to her left and rested her head on his shoulder. "I hope so," she whispered.

She felt Jack brush the top of her head, maybe in a kiss, maybe with his cheek. She didn't know, but it brought comfort to her and she closed her eyes. He wasn't cold now, wasn't pushing her away, but giving her much-needed support. Despite the noise and odor, she felt almost peaceful. They were on their way back, and with any luck, she'd be Alison Sullivan again by tomorrow morning. Then she'd like to introduce herself to Jackson Graham.

The town of Bixby finally came into sight just after three o'clock. And by the time Ali and Jack climbed out of the truck, they were hot, sticky, tired and sick to death of the smell and sound of sheep.

The driver let them out by a service station, then drove off down the main street. Ali stood for a moment inhaling air that wasn't tainted by sheep, then realized that the odor was still there. She looked at Jack, then down at her clothes and tugged the shirt free from her skin to bring it to her nose. The odor permeated everything.

Jack grimaced. "Let's find someplace to buy fresh clothes, then we'll try to find a room. We can get out of sight and find some transportation for the trip tomorrow."

"I've only got about twenty dollars," she said, "and you had to leave the cash deposit at the car rental."

He took out his wallet and looked in it. "Four hundred and seventy-five dollars. We'll make it do." He looked up the street. "We can't just stand here. Let's head up that way and see what we find."

Ali fell in step beside Jack, and they walked down the street, the heat heavy and enervating. They came upon a general store, bought a couple of pairs of jeans, a plain white shirt for him and cotton blouse for her, underwear and toiletries. Jack asked the clerk who rang up their order about motels, and the man told them about a bed-and-breakfast on Madison, a side street near the end of town. He knew the proprietor, a Mrs. Blanco, and he called to find out if there was a vacancy.

He came back, told Jack and Ali she had a room, and then directed them south on the main street. Jack thanked him, then walked out carrying their packages in one hand and holding Ali's hand with the other. "As soon as I get you out of sight, I'll go and find some transportation for tomorrow."

"What are you going to buy?" she asked as they walked quickly through the heat down a street that was almost deserted. "A donkey cart?"

He laughed softly. "You might be closer to the truth than you think."

She cast him a sideways glance, but he was staring straight ahead. When he glanced nervously back over his shoulder and picked up the pace, her smile faltered. "What did you see?"

"Nothing." He looked back at her, his eyes shadowed by the brightness of the sun at his back. "Honestly, nothing. If Will spoke to the right people, Terrine will believe we're about three hundred miles west of here."

"And if he didn't?" she prodded, her steps lagging.

He kept her moving. "We're sitting ducks out here. Let's find Madison Street and get out of sight."

Ali kept going, then spotted a street sign. "There it is," she said, and Jack picked up the pace.

They turned onto a narrow street lined with older homes on sprawling properties. Tufts of grass sprouted in the cracks of the sidewalk, and seed pods from ancient eucalyptus trees were scattered all over the ground. The shade was welcome, and the fragrance of fresh-mowed grass hung in the hot air.

Jack spotted the house partway down the block. "There it is," he said, and headed toward a two-level house that looked like a Spanish hacienda. Two old olive trees shaded the front of the adobe-walled structure and flanked a flagstone walkway that led up to a tiled atrium shut off by a heavy wrought-iron gate.

Ali stayed by Jack up to the gate, then he pushed on the heavy metal and it swung silently back. She and Jack stepped into a three-sided courtyard lined with potted plants and filled with the fragrance of orange blossoms from dwarf trees near the heavy wooden front door. He let go of Ali's hand and approached the door, pressed a doorbell inset in the thick adobe wall. Ali could hear the sound of chimes.

After a moment, the heavy door swung open slowly, and a short woman dressed in a flowing white shift trimmed with bright red embroidery faced them. Her dark skin, dark eyes and raven black hair were a stark contrast to the soft white fabric. As soon as she saw Jack and Ali, she smiled, a broad toothy expression. "Ah, you are the couple who were in the store with Mr. Fletcher?"

"Yes, we're the Jeffers. Mr. Fletcher said you had a room for us."

"Yes, I do." She stood back and motioned them inside. "Welcome, I'm Elena Blanco."

Ali preceded Jack into dim coolness, and as her eyes adjusted, she saw a large living area directly ahead with dark furnishings, clay-tile floors, whitewashed walls and low ceilings crisscrossed by heavy beams.

Spanish-style and tastefully elegant. A curved stair-case to the left led up to the wooden railed balcony of the second floor.

"I have one room available," Mrs. Blanco said as she closed the door.

As Ali turned, she saw the lady sniff faintly, her smile losing a bit of its brilliance. Jack spoke up. "We were in close quarters with a bunch of sheep. I'm afraid they left their mark."

The woman shrugged. "Sheep are smelly animals. There's an adjoining bath to your room, and it's stocked with everything, even perfumed bubble bath. It's seventy-five dollars a night, including dinner and a continental breakfast, payable in advance."

"That sounds fine," Jack said and took out his wallet.

The woman took the money, then motioned them to follow her. She went to the stairway and started up. "It's got a lovely view of the gardens at the back, a pride of my husband's. In this land, to grow anything is a miracle. He has lovely roses." At the top of the stairs, she went to her left and opened a set of double doors.

Ali saw the bedroom, a soft tapestry of pinks, roses, mauves and pale blues. And as Ali slowly entered the room behind Mrs. Blanco, the lovely decorating be-came secondary. The whitewashed walls, French doors at the back framed by heavy draperies, huge armoire and dresser to the left, and sliding doors that revealed a walk-in closet to the right.

All she saw was the bed. A huge four-poster that sat right in the middle of an off-white rug on the hard-wood floor, facing the French doors, with a gauze canopy stretched overhead and a delicate white eyelet spread covering it. A bank of pillows in rose, mauve and blue were arranged on it.

"...and if you need anything else," the woman was saying as she crossed and opened a door that exposed a bathroom with an old-fashioned claw-footed tub, "more towels or blankets, just ask. I'll be downstairs." She came back to where Jack and Ali still stood by the door. "There's dinner if you want it, either up here or in the dining room."

"Up here would be great," Jack said.

"Good. It'll be up at—" she glanced at her watch, then back to Jack "—seven. How's that?"

"Good. I've got to go out for a bit. That'll give me time to take care of business."

"Seven it is, then," Mrs. Blanco said. "Enjoy." She went to the double doors and closed them softly after her.

Ali wandered around the room, wanting so badly to make light of the lone-bed situation, to say something about the Walls of Jericho, but there was no humor left in her. She was weary of the effort of pretending to be Alicia, of pretending to have known Mick Terrine, of pretending to herself that she could walk away from Jack and never look back.

She stopped by the French doors and looked out at the gardens bathed in the richness of the late-afternoon sun. It looked like an oasis, in the middle of this hard unforgiving desert. And she craved that kind of oasis in her life.

"I'll be back in a while," Jack said behind her. "Why don't you make use of the bath and try to get rid of the memory of those sheep?"

She turned to him and couldn't stop herself from saying, "I wish you wouldn't leave."

"I've got to." He took out his wallet and went through it. "I've got to find that donkey cart and hope it doesn't cost any more than about three hundred dollars." He went to the doors and glanced back at Ali. "Lock these and stay in here until I'm back. No roaming around."

"Should I pull the drapes?" she asked, part facetiously, and part worried that she should.

"Good idea," he said, then he was gone and the doors were closed.

She stood alone, the only noise the soft whirring of the ceiling fan. Alone. God, she hated that word. And she had never felt as alone in her life as she did whenever Jack left.

She crossed to the doors, threw the bolt, then turned and hurried to the French doors. She tugged the curtains across to shut out the glow of twilight, then went into the bathroom. Once she started the hot water in the bathtub, she found the bubble bath and poured a cap of the pink liquid into the water. As it foamed, she stripped off her dirty clothes, dropped them in a pile on the floor and stepped into the steamy bath. The sensation of slipping into the heat, fragrant with lilacs, and sliding down until the bubbles were up to her chin was wonderful. She closed her eyes, and for a few moments she could make believe that life was normal.

Half an hour later, when Ali was out of the tub and dressed in clean clothes, Jack still wasn't back. She brushed at her hair, settled with getting it back off her face, then went into the bedroom. She snapped on a couple of side lights to banish the gathering shadows and sank onto the edge of the bed. Wiggling her bare toes into the softness of the rug, she looked at the phone on the nightstand. For a moment her need to make connection with home was staggering. If she could just talk to Lydia or Alicia . . .

She began to reach for the receiver, but a knock on the door stopped her. She turned and stared at the door, then let out a sigh of relief when she heard Jack say, "It's me, Ali. Open up."

She scrambled off the bed and hurried across to throw the bolt and pull open the door. The sight of Jack, perspiration sheening his skin, his clothes sticking to him, even that clinging odor of sheep, were so welcome she could feel tears pricking her eyes. She was tired and overextended emotionally, she told herself. That was why she had the urge to throw herself into his arms and hold on for dear life.

He was carrying a large tray covered by a blue linen cloth. "Mrs. Blanco caught me at the front door and gave me this to bring up." He crossed and set the tray on the table in front of the French doors, then turned to Ali. His eyes skimmed over her, and she thought she saw a flicker of appreciation before he looked away and started to take off his shoes. "If you're done in the bathroom, I could use it."

"I'm all done," she said. "Did you find anything?"

He glanced up at her as he stepped out of his shoes. "Yes, and it only cost two hundred and seventy-five dollars."

"A donkey cart?"

He flashed her a weak smile. "Not quite, but it might turn into a pumpkin at midnight. It's got a hundred and fifty thousand miles on it. Let's hope it has one trip to Las Vegas left in it." He started for the bath. "I'll be out in a bit."

When the bathroom door closed, Ali moved to the table and took the cloth off the tray. Her stomach rumbled when she saw two plates filled with chicken salad, fresh vegetables, fruit wedges and cheese. A small carafe of white wine and two glasses were to the side, along with a basket of crusty rolls.

Ali glanced at the closed bathroom door, heard the water start and decided not to wait for Jack. She was starving. She sat down, poured a glass of wine and found the silverware. The food tasted delicious, and it wasn't long before more than half of her plate was empty. She picked up a roll, tore it into halves and nibbled on one as she sat back in the chair. Then she stood and went to the French doors.

Carefully she nudged back the heavy curtains just enough to see the night outside. Day was completely gone. Darkness blanketed the land. Slowly she let the curtains fall back into place. She crossed to the table, looked down at her partially eaten dinner, then dropped the piece of roll onto her plate. Her hunger was gone.

She moved restlessly around the room, aware of the silence in the bathroom. Then she went back to the bed. She sat on the edge and, clasping her hands in her lap, stared at the bathroom door, willing Jack to come back into the room.

She didn't want to be alone like this. She didn't want this sense of being cut off from everything. Then she noticed the phone again. If she could only know that Lydia was all right, that Alicia was with her and that Alicia would be back tomorrow, she'd feel so much better.

She reached out and touched the receiver, felt the cool plastic under her hand, then impulsively she picked it up. She shifted closer, put the phone to her ear and started to dial the number of the hospital in Los Angeles. Before she could hit more than two numbers, Jack was in the room and coming toward her.

For a moment she had a flashback of when he tackled her in the hotel room when she'd been shot at, but the instant she looked up at his face, she knew this was different. Anger was etched in his face, and he grabbed the receiver from her, jerking it free of her hold, and slammed it down on the cradle so hard that the sound echoed in the room.

"What in the hell are you up to?" he demanded.

She drew back, every bit as aware of the fact he was wearing only a towel as she was of the anger that radiated from him. "I ... I was going to ... to ..."

"To what? Let someone know where we are?"

"Why would—" She bit her lip and drew her hands back to clutch them in her lap. "I wouldn't ..."

He stood over her. "Who did you call last time?"

"What time?"

"When you were with Lucy? Who did you call?"

She couldn't keep eye contact. "I didn't call anyone."

"I might have known."

She looked back up at him. "What?"

"Lies. They come easily to you, don't they?"

His hair was still damp, and his skin flushed from the heat of the bathwater. Probably flushed from anger, too, she thought. She wanted to say she didn't lie, but after this weekend that would hardly be the truth. "All right. I was going to call someone who's in the hospital. I was just worried."

He studied her as if he didn't quite know what to make of her. "A sick friend?"

"A special person," she whispered, and looked down.

He cupped her chin and made her look back at him. "Who is he?"

She could feel the tension in his touch, that unsteadiness as if he were containing an anger that could shatter the world. But as she met his gaze, she felt confused. There was anger there, yet she could have sworn there was a shadow of pain. She didn't understand that at all. "There...isn't anyone. Not like that."

"No new Mick Terrine waiting in the wings?"

She touched her tongue to her lips. *There's just you,* she thought before she could stop herself. And she knew it was the truth. This man. He was everything right now. "I never..." She bit her lip, hoping to keep it steady. "Mick Terrine was never anyone important."

His hold on her chin tightened for a moment, then he jerked his hand away. "That's pathetic."

"What is?" she asked, making herself not touch the spot where he'd held her.

"You just used Mick Terrine for what he was, what he had, what he could do for you. Now that he's out of circulation, you'll move on to bigger and better conquests. That's pathetic and disgusting.''

Thanks to her lies and pretending, he thought she was shallow and had lots of men. That she attracted men like the Terrines, used them, then moved on. If she told him the truth, he'd probably laugh in her face. And that thought hurt so much she could barely breathe. He couldn't even touch her without feeling disgust.

She stood, needing to get away, to put some distance between them and maybe find a reprieve from the thoughts that were hammering at her. But Jack didn't move, and she found herself bumping into him. For a moment he steadied her with both hands on her shoulders, and his face was so close that when he inhaled she felt as if he were taking the soul right out of her.

How could she love a man like this?

Love?

She stared at Jack, searching his face, desperate for a denial, for something to cling to that would wipe out the clarity of that single thought. But nothing came. Nothing at all. Love. It was here, now, with this man, and she had never known it before. The feeling was new, stunning . . . terrifying.

She ducked her head, trying to will her legs to move, but her body seemed incapable of making the escape to the bathroom.

"Ali?" Jack said in a rough whisper.

She stared down, but that only backfired when she saw the towel at his hips, the bare stomach, the strong legs. Closing her eyes, she didn't even dare breathe. "What?"

"Who were you going to call?"

She shook her head, so weary of the life she'd led this weekend that she could barely make herself say the words. "I can't tell you."

"Why?"

"Because."

"Just because?"

She nodded without looking up.

"That's no answer." His hands on her were as binding as bands of steel. "I need to know."

She kept her eyes closed so tightly that color exploded behind her lids. "Why?"

The world seemed to stop, and reality centered on the man touching her. All she heard was her own heart hammering and Jack's rough breathing. All she felt was his hands on her and his body heat, which ran the length of her.

His hold tightened. "Tell me, Ali."

She took a painful breath and made herself look up at him. There were no more lies in her, nothing to fabricate a story from, but she couldn't tell him the truth. She didn't know what to say or what to do, but when she met his deep blue gaze, all thoughts were gone. Pure instinct took over, melding with a love for this man that shook her, and she touched his chest.

Her fingertips pressed against the sprinkling of hair, felt the dampness of his skin, the beating of his heart, the tension in each breath he took. Then she moved closer, and as Jack muttered an oath that was low and harsh, she lifted her hand to his chin. Her finger touched the scar, felt the knotted smoothness and, before she understood what she was going to do, she raised herself on her toes and pressed her lips to the scar.

She felt his sharp intake of air, then she was acting on an instinct as old as time, an instinct that surely came from being human. She'd had no teaching sessions, no weeks or months of practice, but as his head lowered to hers, her arms wrapped around his neck, and her body strained to his as her lips parted, inviting his invasion.

There was no hesitation in Jack. His mouth had hers, slanting over it, his lips hot and demanding, his tongue invading her with quick sure strokes. Rational thoughts be damned. Thoughts of everyone and everything else were gone. No questions, no hesitations. In a heartbeat, Ali made the biggest decision of her life. She would give herself to Jack.

She clung to him, arching her body to fit the angles of his strong frame, shocking herself by tugging him back toward the bed. Together they fell onto the soft spread, and Jack was over her, his weight a welcome burden, his lips tracing a path of fire from her lips to her chin, then to the hollow of her throat.

When his hands tugged at her blouse, she fumbled with the buttons, pushing the white cotton aside. Then the flimsy lace of her bra was gone, the front hook unsnapped in a heartbeat, and his hands found her breasts. The contact overwhelmed her, the messages the touch ran through her body, bombarding her from all sides.

She ached at the same time she thrilled at the sensations of the contact. Her breasts swelled, straining to his touch, then his lips replaced his hands, and Ali knew a burst of ecstasy that literally took her breath away. She arched upward, her head thrown back, and her fingers buried in Jack's thick hair. His tongue teased and taunted her nipples, first one then the other, until they were hard buds of pleasure.

Fragmenting into a million shards of pleasure seemed a probability, and when his hand spanned her stomach, then slipped lower, she knew it was a certainty. She helped Jack slip off her jeans, then her panties, and she knew no embarrassment. When Jack drew back, gazing down at her, she saw the passion in his eyes, the desire that deepened the blue to smoke and fire. And as his hands skimmed over her, stopping to tease her, to caress her, then move to another spot where the glory and pleasure only increased, she saw pure need in his eyes. And that need was a living thing in her.

And she wanted him. She wanted to see him, to touch him, to feel the evidence of his need for her. Tugging the towel from around him, she gasped at the sight of him. Then slowly and gently, Jack took her hand, easing it toward him until she found his strength.

His groan echoed all around her, and when her hand moved, when her fingers circled and caressed him, she knew that this moment had been inevitable since the first time she set eyes on Jack Graham. Inevitable and as important to her as her next breath.

"Are you sure?" Jack asked in a rough unsteady voice.

"Yes," she whispered. "Are you?"

Chapter 11

Jack had never felt so sure of anything in his life. No doubts, no fears, he simply wanted Ali and he wanted her now. He wanted to be one with her, to be in her and to know her in the most intimate way.

"Very sure," he said, watching the flush of passion, the soft parting of her lips, lips bruised from his own kisses. His hand trailed over her stomach, splaying to feel the soft roundness, then moving lower to her feminine center. His finger found the bud, swollen and so sensitive that she cried out when he made contact.

When he moved, stroking the swollen heat, her whimpers inflamed him, her rapid breathing echoing his own. Then he felt the moistness, that readiness in her that told him she was prepared to take him. Part of him wanted it and wanted it now, without any hesitation, and another part knew that what was about to

happen would be special and so unique that it was to
be savored.

Using all his willpower, he didn't move. He let his
hands know her, let his fingers invade her, pressed the
heel of his hand to her pelvic bone. Slowly he moved
in and out, feeling her small spasms, hearing her soft
cries. His lips touched her throat as she threw back her
head, and he knew she was on the brink. But he didn't
want it like this. He wanted to be in her when the
world exploded for her, and he wanted to be with her
every step of the way.

When he withdrew, he felt her hand find his, and he
looked down at her. "Please," she whispered,
"please, love me," and he did. He moved over her,
touched her moist heat with his strength, testing her,
absorbing the shock of white-hot passion that en-
compassed him. He ceased movement for a moment,
letting sensations focus, to stop his own fragmenting,
then he slowly pushed against her.

The surge of feelings centered in his soul. The sensations engulfed him, growing and growing, her small
shock waves against him driving him to want more and
more. Then he was in her, and he knew something in
that instant that robbed him of all thought. The idea
was there, the realization so clear that it hurt, but then
it was gone before he could hold on to it and know it.
He was in her, surrounded by a sweetness that ripped
at his soul. And when he moved, when he plunged into
her, when he felt her nipples harden against his chest,
heard her low cries for more, he let himself go.

To cherish someone was breathtaking. To care so
much that it hurt was monumental, and to know that
you had touched the soul of that person almost took

the life out of his body. He rose higher and higher with
Ali, felt her keep time with him, felt her hands grasp
the knotted muscles in his back, then lower to his but-
tocks, pulling him into her with more and more focus.

Then the moment came, flared into reality, consuming him in a way that was cleansing, yet replen-
ishing, as if finding this zenith would only give him
more life and more pleasure. He shot higher and
higher, felt Ali going with him, then the pleasure was
everywhere. The joy and happiness was eternal, and
as Ali cried out, he heard his voice echoing hers, and
he knew that he'd found that part of his soul that he
hadn't even known was missing until this very heartbeat.

He eased himself back, leaving her, but not letting
go of her. Angling his body at her side, he pulled her
to him, and she trustingly rested her head over his
heart, her hair tickling his chin. Her leg rested over his
thigh, her hand relaxed on his stomach. He felt her
take a shaky breath, then release it on a trembling sigh
and lie against him.

His fingers tangled in her rich hair, his other hand
rested in the swell of her hip. He felt the euphoria
shifting, drifting slowly away, replaced by a sense of
satisfaction that was working its way deep into his being. This was a first for him, to feel as if he should
stay, as if he wanted to stay for the rest of his life right
where he was now. A first.

His heart clenched and everything shifted. He knew
now what he'd found during their lovemaking, the
thing that had eluded him in the heat of passion, but

something that stunned and thrilled him all at once. Ali had been a virgin.

She sighed, and he felt her move closer, snuggling into his side with a gesture of trust that made his heart catch. It didn't make sense. No woman who was in a room with Mick Terrine for more than ten minutes would have left a virgin. He skimmed his hand over the curve of her hip, the sensations of silky warmth under his touch making his body tighten.

Ali had never been with any other man.

The thought sank in, settling somewhere between wonder and confusion. Will had told him Ali claimed she and Mick were just acquaintances. But Jack had never bought that—not until now. He just didn't understand how it could be. He needed to know. His hand on her hip stilled, and he rubbed his chin on the veil of her hair. "Ali?"

"Mmm?" she breathed, the action sending a ripple along his side.

"Are you okay?"

She nodded, her hair tickling his chin. "Just fine," she whispered, her breath warm on his chest. "No. I'm better than fine. I..." She traced a finger lightly up his chest, pressing it to the hollow of his throat. "I don't remember ever feeling like this."

The simplicity of her words hit him hard, and he closed his eyes. There had been women in his life, some staying longer than others, but in truth, he couldn't remember one of them ever making him feel the way Ali had.

She shifted, her lips pressing to his skin, and he couldn't stop the groan that seemed to come up from the soles of his feet. He turned to face her, the angles and curves of her body fitting so neatly with his that he wouldn't have questioned anyone if they told him he and Ali had been created just to lie like this. Forever.

He opened his eyes and found her looking up at him, her gaze heavy with desire, the same desire flaring to life in him. She gently touched his face, her fingers caressing his jaw, then the warmth of her palm pressing his cheek.

It shocked him that desire could come so quickly and so fiercely. To have it rob him of all thought and reason. The fire flared white-hot, and when his mouth found hers, the world narrowed to two people. It existed for this moment, as surely as he had been looking for Ali all his life. That thought was staggering, yet so clear to him that he didn't doubt its truth.

He tasted her, felt her, and when she offered herself to him, he took her with a sense of thanksgiving he'd never before felt. He filled her and knew her, and would have willingly given all he possessed for her to experience a fraction of the joy he had experienced right then. She moved, she gave, she was everything in his world.

And when the ultimate joy came, when the tidal wave of ecstasy washed over him, he heard Ali's name echoing, knew it was his voice, knew it was stamped on his soul. A heartbeat later, she convulsed around him, his pleasure in that so intense that he knew what it meant to feel pain on the same plane as joy.

And he was filled with a sense of rightness that blotted out everything. But as the feelings mellowed, as the shards of pleasure dissipated, as Ali and he settled in languid contentment, the world began to nudge at him. And the fact that Ali was a virgin wouldn't stop coming to him. As soft silence filled the room, as he felt her snuggling against him, he knew he had to understand.

"Life never ceases to surprise me," he murmured.

She spread her hand on his chest and her fingers teased his skin, tracing the irregular path of the scar at his shoulder. "Me, too."

"What are you surprised about?"

"Everything. This. Me. You."

He laughed softly. "That about says it all."

"What are you surprised about?" she asked.

He had his opening, the chance to say something, but he had to force the words out. "I had no idea you were a virgin."

Her hand stilled on him, and when she spoke, he knew that he'd gone about this all wrong. "It was that obvious?"

He was a jerk. "No, I mean, yes, but..."

"I'm sorry," she whispered.

God, there was nothing to apologize for. She'd been more wonderful than a woman with years of experience, and the joy of knowing he was the first man to be with her was something he couldn't begin to put into words. "I just meant, it doesn't make sense."

"What doesn't?" she murmured as she shifted, her hand drawing back to rest in a loose fist between them.

The contact wasn't broken, but he could feel a distance between them that had little to do with physical positioning. His instincts were to shut up, to pull her back to him and forget the whole thing, but he couldn't. He had to understand. Either she was the first totally honest person he'd ever met and she *had* been only friends with Terrine, or— Or what?

He could tell she was staring at the ceiling, and her breathing was quick and shallow. "You've been with Mick Terrine. He doesn't have friends. He has lovers."

"I was never *with* Mick Terrine," she said, her voice flat. "He never touched me. I told you that."

He was the one to draw back this time, shifting to raise himself on one elbow to look down at her to see if she was joking. But he could tell she was dead serious. She looked at him, her eyes shadowed, but he could see tension in her expression. "Never?"

"Never," she echoed, not looking at him. "Not even a kiss."

She might not have slept with Terrine, but one thing he knew with certainty—Terrine was totally heterosexual, and no man could be this close to Ali and not want her. "I don't want lies, not now," he said, knowing the gut-wrenching truth of those words. After making love to her, the thought of lies tore at him.

"Neither do I," she said, and rolled to her right and away from him. She tugged the sheet with her as she sat up, her legs over the side of the bed, her naked back to Jack. "I don't want to lie to you anymore, but—"

"Then don't," he said.

She took a breath and he could see her shoulders tremble. "You have to promise me you won't do anything if I tell you the truth."

The sleek lines of her bare back taunted him. "Do what?" he asked, willing himself not to touch her and trail his finger down her spine.

"Anything, at least not until I can explain everything."

He sat up, not caring that the sheets slid off him. What in the hell was she talking about? For a moment he wondered if he'd been wrong, that she hadn't been a virgin. Then he knew that wasn't possible. "What's going on?"

She cast him a look back over her shoulder, her eyes dark, her hair tumbling around her face. "Promise me you'll listen and won't act until I've explained."

"I don't give blind promises. I—"

"Forget it. I shouldn't have said anything," she muttered, and would have stood if Jack hadn't reached and pulled her by the arm, jerking her around. All the mellow feelings were gone, and his nerves felt raw.

"Hey, what's going on?"

She froze, the only motion the rapid rise and fall of her chest.

Jack moved closer to her, letting go of her arm so he could catch her by her shoulders. He turned her around, and in a tangle of sheets she faced him, her expression filled with such pain he was stunned. The need to soothe her pain, to bring back the glow of passion, overwhelmed him, but when he would have drawn her to him, she stiffened and resisted.

With his hands still on her shoulders, he studied her, then let her go. He sat back and met Ali's gaze. Pain? Yes. But more. And he felt fear growing in him. There was something basically wrong, something that hadn't existed moments ago. And he'd be damned if he knew what it could be.

Ali had the sheet clutched tightly to her breasts. Her hair curled around her face, a face that seemed unnaturally pale, and her tongue darted out to touch her parted lips. One thing he did know. He couldn't sit here when the beauty he knew all too well, hidden with just a flimsy sheet, was within inches of his reach. Not if he wanted to stay sane. And something in him knew he'd need all that sanity for what she was going to tell him.

He moved away and got off the bed. Without looking at Ali, he headed for the bathroom. "I'll be right back." And he went in search of clothes before he returned in search of the truth.

Ali couldn't watch Jack cross to the bathroom. She couldn't see the strong lines of his body and remember how, for a moment in time, she'd felt fused with him. She felt as if her soul blended with his, that she had once and forever been a complete person. But that had been an illusion born out of the love she had for him. The same love that meant she had to tell him the truth.

She didn't want him to think of her as Alicia. She didn't want to playact with Jack. She couldn't. Not after she had totally exposed her innermost person to him just minutes ago. That truth she'd experienced was something no one had ever told her about when they spoke of "making love" or "having sex." No one had told her that all pretenses, all make-believe, all lies, were stripped away, and for those moments, she'd understood complete truth. Terrifying and thrilling at the same moment.

And she knew the one person she wanted to keep that with, to protect it with, was Jack. She heard the

door click shut, and she moved quickly, finding her
clothes and tugging on her blouse and jeans. She was
just buttoning the waistband when Jack came back
into the room.

In the low light she turned, and the sight of him with
the brightness of the bathroom light at his back literally took her breath away. Jeans. That's all he had on.
Light flared out from behind him, defining his broad
shoulders, his narrow hips, and the glow shimmered
on his skin. He reached to one side, flicked off the
bathroom light, and everything softened with shadows at the perimeter, the low glow from the side lamp
gentling the picture.

No one had told her that loving a person would be
so painful.

She stood by the bed, waiting, then he came toward
her, the low light shading his eyes. "All right," he
said. "I won't do anything until you explain whatever
the hell you've got to explain."

Now was her chance, but she found it almost impossible to sort through her thoughts, to find one coherent sentence that could begin the explanation. She
lowered herself onto the edge of the bed and stared
down at the hands clenched in her lap. "I'm not Alicia Sullivan."

She braced herself, not sure if there would be an
explosion, either physically or verbally, but none
came. Jack uttered one word. "What?"

"I'm not Alicia." She took another breath and
forced out the words. "I'm her sister, her twin."

Then contact came. He grasped her shoulders,
pulling her to her feet as if she didn't weigh more than

a feather. But she didn't meet his gaze. "What in the hell are you talking about?" he demanded.

"I'm Alison Sullivan."

The room fell into heavy silence as Jack assimilated what Ali was saying. Then everything fell into place. Her likes and dislikes, her attitude about things, her lack of knowledge of the Terrines—and her virginity. Sourness rose in the back of his throat. It was lies, all lies. And he'd bought them, hook, line and sinker.

He let her go, unable to bear the feel of her under his hands, and she stumbled backward onto the bed. He had to think, and touching her was a way to guarantee those thoughts would be a jumble of confusion and lingering desire. "What kind of game is this?"

She looked up at him as she sat up on the bed, her hands again clenched into tight fists. "It's no game."

"What is it?" he demanded, thankful that he was beginning to sharpen, and the haze of the last hour was almost gone.

"It's...it's..." Her words trailed off and her teeth worried her bottom lip. She took a shaky breath, then words began to tumble out. He heard about her foster mother, her sister's phone call, their agreement to trade places and the switch in the courthouse washroom. "And Alicia said all I had to do was stay in a hotel room for the weekend while she visited Lydia." She laughed, but the sound ended on a sob. "A nice safe weekend. What a joke."

Her words produced an anger in him that almost made him shake. A charade. A childish prank. And he'd fallen for it. Damn it all to hell, he'd fallen for it like some adolescent with raging hormones! He turned from her and crossed to the French doors. He didn't bother pulling back the curtains. No view would make things better.

Then he knew how deeply he'd allowed Ali's lies to affect him. All he was thinking about was himself, the wrenching feeling in his gut, the pain at being used, then the real stakes hit him. Alicia Sullivan was on the loose and the case against Mick Terrine was in shambles.

He turned back to Ali. She was still on the bed watching him. The fact that she looked so small and vulnerable was pushed aside as he strode back to the bed. He stood over her. "Where in the hell is your sister right now?"

"I told you—seeing Lydia before the surgery."

"Where?" he bit out.

Ali flinched at his tone, but she stood to face him. "With Lydia."

He backed up slightly to keep from making any contact with her. One touch, and he wouldn't be responsible for his actions. "And where is Lydia?"

"In the hospital. I told you she's going to have surgery soon, and she—"

"Enough." He held up both hands palms out in her direction, giving himself the illusion of warding her off. "Stop this. You know what I want to know."

Ali narrowed her eyes, trying to dull the clarity of the image of Jack in front of her. She didn't want to see the intensity in his eyes, or the anger that thinned his mouth. She knew what he wanted to know, and there was no way she could tell him. She didn't want Lydia to endure the shock, and she sure didn't want the Terrines to know anything about Lydia or Los Angeles. If the Terrines were trying to kill Alicia, they wouldn't think twice about hurting anyone else. "I can't tell you."

"You sure as hell better," he ground out, his hands dropping to curl into fists at his sides.

She never should have told him anything. She never should have acted on such a selfish plane. Just because she thought it would make her feel better to be honest with him, she shouldn't have. Now everything was at stake. "Alicia's going to be back to change places tomorrow morning. She'll be there to testify in front of the grand jury."

"And you believed her?"

"Of course. She promised me, and she doesn't lie."

"I guess she's not exactly like you, then, is she?" His tone cut her to her soul. "You haven't told the truth for so long I doubt you'd even recognize it if it leapt up and struck you in the face." He turned from her and reached for the phone.

Panic choked Ali, and she dove at Jack, grasping his hand before he could touch the receiver. He stopped, but she knew it wasn't because he thought she could physically make him do so. He stopped because he knew he could place a call any time he wanted to. And he would, unless she could talk him out of it.

Her hand held tightly to his, and he didn't pull free. Instead, he took a step toward her, and she could feel the heat of his body penetrating her clothes. As she looked up, the lover she had known just minutes ago was gone. Hard, cold blue eyes drilled into her, and she was the one to retreat. She drew back, pushing her hands behind her, and she had to force herself not to beg Jack to give Alicia a chance to come back on her own.

"I know you don't have any reason to trust me." A flashing of a sarcastic smile touched his lips, and her heart sank. She wished he could have a fraction of the trust in her that she had in him. That trust had been the reason she'd made love with him.

She knew Jack Graham was a good man. He was honest and solid. He hated Mick Terrine, and he hated lies. She knew that he thought she'd blown everything for the case against Terrine. And he hated that. Despite what had happened between them, he hated her. That thought hurt more than anything ever had.

She swallowed hard, trying to ease the tightness in her throat. "I just want you to believe that what I'm saying is true. Alicia will be there tomorrow morning."

"And if she's not?"

She didn't have an answer for that. All she knew was that if Jack made that call and Alicia's name and picture splashed all over the news, it would destroy everyone, including Lydia. And Alicia wouldn't have a hope of surviving the Terrine's actions. "You…you can do anything you want to me. I'll take whatever's coming."

"And that's going to make Mick Terrine pay for what he did?"

"No, of course not," she admitted, her stomach aching horribly. She pressed a hand to her middle and tried to regroup. "What's going to happen if you make that call?"

"Will can put out an APB on your sister."

"Even if they do that, it won't do any good. It'll take time to work, and by then, the grand jury will have already convened. Can't you just give her the chance to come back, to make the switch again, and if she isn't there, I'll tell you anything you want to know? Believe me, I'll take you to her personally if she doesn't show up."

Jack wasn't used to having to think twice about what was right or wrong. At any other time he would have made the call and damned the consequences. But as Ali looked up at him, her green eyes shadowed by those ridiculously long lashes, he knew she was right. An APB wouldn't have a chance of getting results for a day, maybe even more.

He hated it, but he knew right then that his only hope was that Alicia really would be back to make the switch. He pushed his hands into the pockets of his jeans and rocked forward on the balls of his feet. "I don't have a choice. I'll give her a chance to come back, but so help me, if she's not there, you've opened yourself up to charges."

She shrugged, a fluttery lifting of her shoulders. "I know that. I don't care. Not now. As long as Lydia is okay and Alicia gets back to testify, that's all that matters."

He studied her, and a pure anger wrenched him. And it had little to do with Mick Terrine. It was centered on Ali. She'd been an illusion. He'd held that illusion, touched her, explored her and loved her. That thought brought him up short, and he felt a spasm in his stomach.

Love? He stared at her and almost laughed out loud. He'd never even known what love could be until now, and he'd fallen in love with a woman who didn't even exist.

Chapter 12

Crane didn't hear them until it was too late. He'd gone onto his porch to call the dogs, the darkness of night all around, and just as he turned to go back inside, he heard a footfall. Before he could turn to see who was there, he felt a shattering impact just above his left ear.

The world exploded into star bursts and streaks of red, then he'd passed out. When he came around, he was in a straight-backed chair in the middle of his living room. His hands were tied behind the chair, the cord cutting into his wrists, and his legs had been tied at the ankles to the chair legs.

When he opened his eyes, he wasn't surprised to see the bald man Jack had called Sharp standing in front of him, slowly putting on black leather gloves. The other man was methodically searching the room.

Sharp looked as if he was going to smile, then bent over to bring his face inches from Crane's.

"Glad you're awake. We've got some talking to do, you and me."

Crane looked around, trying to see where the dogs were, then he heard a howling. "They're locked in the barn. It's just us," the bald man said.

Crane didn't say a thing, just looked at him and waited.

"Listen to me, and listen good, old man. I want the girl." He held the black-and-white picture he'd shown Crane the first time he'd come past, and brought it within inches of his face. "This girl. I want her now."

Crane knew that everything Jack had told him was true. But that didn't surprise him. Something about the two young people had made him offer his home to them, let them stay for the night and even offer them his truck. He blinked, clearing his vision, and knew that this man in front of him was basically a coward. If he had you trussed up like a stuck pig, he was overpowering, but Crane bet that in a one-on-one the bald man would fold real easy. Too bad his hands were tied so damned tight.

"Where did she go?" the bald man asked.

Crane shook his head. "I told you last night. I dropped them at the—"

The gloved hand stung Crane's face, cutting off his words and snapping his head to the right. He tasted blood on his tongue.

"Don't lie to me, old man. We know they were here last night. They left this morning. I want to know where they went."

"Sharp?" The other man called to his associate. "Look at this."

Sharp crossed the room, and Crane twisted to see the two men at the phone. Sharp took something off the top of the wall phone. "Money. Maybe somebody made a call."

Sharp looked at the phone, then lifted the receiver and pushed the redial button. He listened, then smiled, a cold cutting expression, then hung the phone back up. Silently he came back to Crane and sank to his haunches in front of him. The smile was still in place. "All right. He was here. He contacted that cop friend of his in Vegas. Now, you tell me what they were driving when they left."

Crane exhaled. Lying wouldn't work, so he figured the truth was vague enough to give Jack and Ali a decent shot at making it to court tomorrow. "I offered them my truck, but they refused it. They said they'd hitch a ride." He couldn't resist a small lie. "The guy said he'd stay on the back roads and they could work their way back."

Sharp studied Crane for a long moment, then got to his feet. "When did they leave?"

"Sunup. They was in a real hurry, just waiting for light, then they took off." When Sharp shifted, Crane saw the gun tucked in a shoulder holster. *Could be the end of everything,* he thought, but that didn't scare him much. A lot of years had passed. A lot of empty years. If this guy thought showing him the gun would make him plead and cry, he was way wrong. Crane didn't particularly want to die, but he wasn't about to give someone like this guy any satisfaction.

"Where did they say they were going?"

Crane knew that a lie here wasn't going to be any use to anyone, not even Jack. "Vegas. They had to be there tomorrow morning."

Sharp stared at him long and hard, then nodded to his cohort. The next thing Crane knew, the phone had been ripped off the wall and tossed onto the floor. Sharp touched his gun, but it didn't leave the holster. "We're leaving, and if I was you, old man, I'd forget this ever happened. Benny's taking a few wires out of your truck. So by the time you can get to anyone, it'll be too late." Then he was gone.

Crane sank back in his chair, listened to the car start, then drive off. When the engine sound faded into the distance, he muttered a violent oath that he hadn't needed to use for years. Then, methodically, he began to rub the rope that bound his wrists against the corner of the wooden seat.

Jack had spent the night in the chaise longue by the windows, trying his damnedest to shut out the one thing that seemed bent on claiming all of his attention. Ali in the bed. She seldom moved, made few noises, but he knew she hadn't slept much, either. And when dawn finally broke, she got up and silently went into the bathroom.

Jack stood, stretching his arms over his head to try to ease the kinks in his muscles, then moved to the French doors. Parting the heavy curtains just enough to look out, he saw the world blanketed in the clear light of morning.

In two days, his world had fallen apart, and for the first time in his life, Jack had no idea how to fix it.

Studies for the bar exam had fallen by the wayside, as had any rational grip he'd had on his own existence.

He fingered the scar on his chin, the past nudging the present, the same way the previous night nudged this new day. There was so much at stake, and Jack had no control over anything, least of all himself.

He heard water running in the bathroom and knew Ali was taking a bath. Images came in that instant, images of her naked body sleek with water, her full breasts, the flare of her hips.

"No control at all," he muttered as he crossed the room to the double doors, opened them and went out onto the landing. He headed down the spiral staircase. Only when he was in the cool dimness of the ground-floor rooms, with distance between himself and Ali did he feel as if he could focus. Get to the city, get Ali to the rest room, hope and pray her twin was waiting for the exchange, then see that Mick paid the price.

"Mr. Jeffers?" He turned and saw Mrs. Blanco approaching. "Thought I heard someone coming down. When will you be wanting breakfast?"

He pushed his hands into his pockets, thankful the light down here wasn't good. Maybe she couldn't see that he looked like hell. He knew he felt like hell. "Could we have it to go?"

"No problem. When?"

"In half an hour. We need to get on the road."

She came closer, and as her eyes narrowed, he knew she got her first good look at him. But she didn't say a thing about it. "How about some fruit, and croissants with ham?"

The idea of eating anything made Jack feel sick, but he nodded. "I'll get it on our way out."

"And I'll have it ready," she said, then turned and went into the kitchen.

Jack knew he had to go back upstairs but hated the idea of it. His nerves were shot, and he felt as if he was perched on a narrow fence. If he fell one way, he'd let himself care about Ali and probably perish. If he went the other way, there would never be an Ali in his life again. And maybe he'd perish, anyway. He headed for the stairs and started up. He didn't know which was a more horrible scenario.

Ali came out of the bathroom and was incredibly relieved that Jack wasn't there. Bad enough she'd spent an unbearable night knowing he was within arm's reach, so close she could hear his breathing, but she couldn't touch him. She found her shoes and socks and sat on the bed to put them on, then looked around.

How could everything else look the same when she felt as if she had changed completely? How could life alter and shift, without there being some real evidence beyond the horrible ache behind her breastbone? She didn't understand anything anymore except the need for her to get back and change places with Alicia.

She closed her eyes for a moment and prayed earnestly that Lydia was going to be all right and that Alicia was going to be waiting for her at the courthouse. Then the door clicked open, and she jumped, turning to see Jack come back into the room.

He looked haggard, as if he hadn't slept any better than she had. Yet she wondered if any man had ever looked more seductive with mussed hair, the shadow of new beard darkening his jaw, his lean body indecently visible above the jeans. He moved quietly without saying a word and without looking at her. Then he disappeared into the bathroom. As the door shut behind him, Ali sank back on the bed and looked at the clock. Six-fifteen.

A new day, a day of hope—so why did she feel as if she was facing her own execution?

The car Jack bought was actually pretty decent. It was old, with oxidized blue paint and torn upholstery, but it had an efficient air conditioner, bucket seats that were reasonably comfortable, and the engine started on the first try. But it was way too small. As Ali settled in the front seat, she leaned as far away from Jack as she could and ignored the breakfast that Mrs. Blanco had put together for them. Food was the least of her concerns at the moment.

For miles there was nothing but silence in the car, and when Jack spoke, the sound of his voice gave her a start. "Let's get some things straight."

For a moment she thought he wanted to talk about what had happened with them, that there was a chance to straighten them out, but one look at Jack and she knew how incredibly foolish that thought was. He was looking directly ahead, his jaw tight, his expression grim.

"All right," she said.

"We'll be at the courthouse in half an hour. Before we approach it, I'm going to stop and call Will to get a clearance. You'll get on the floor, stay down until I tell you otherwise. We'll go to the back secured entrance, the one we left by on Friday. When the car stops, I'll tell you when to get out. I want you to slide over the seat and use my door, and once you're out, don't stop. Get to the door and get inside."

"Can I make it to the rest room without a problem?"

"I'll be sure you do." He slanted her a look, the blue of his eyes as cold as chipped ice. "You just make sure the switch happens."

"Are you going to tell anyone?"

His eyes narrowed on the road ahead. "That depends."

"On what?"

"If your sister's there, if she testifies and if Mick Terrine gets put away, I don't see why anyone needs to know anything. But if it's blown . . ." He let his words trail off, the implication so strong that Ali felt her stomach tighten.

She looked away from Jack and saw the skyline of the city off in the distance. "We aren't really identical, you know," she said.

"What?"

Las Vegas got nearer and nearer. "We're mirror twins. When I look at Alicia, it's as if I'm looking in a mirror. Lydia was the only one who could tell us apart." She clasped and unclasped her hands in her lap. "We could never fool her—at least, not for long."

"Then she's one of the lucky ones," he muttered, and turned off the freeway. At the end of the off ramp, he swung right into a gas station and pulled up to a series of pay phones. He got out, leaving the car idling, and went into one. Ali watched him make a call, then come back to the car.

As he got in, he said without looking at her, "It's all set. Will's got it cleared for us." He put the car in gear and backed up, then headed for the on ramp. As he drove onto the freeway, he said, "With any luck, this will all be over in a short while."

With any luck it would be settled and finished, but Ali knew, for her, that was far from the truth. What she had to look forward to was a life of regrets, of finding love and having it destroyed while she watched. And she'd done it all herself.

"Jack?"

"What?"

"I need to say something before we get there."

He slowed the car a little and glanced at her, his eyes direct and cutting. "I don't need another lesson in twins."

"No, it's not that."

"Well, if you've lied about anything else, you'd better tell me now."

She flinched at the tone of his voice. "No lies. I just need to explain."

"Explain what?"

"About why I did this. You never asked me last night."

The car sped up. As he moved into the fast lane, he said, "You told me. Your sister asked you to do it so she could go and see your mother."

"My foster mother, Lydia."

"And you took her place, lied, put this whole case in jeopardy, and you feel justified." He drove even faster. "The one thing you haven't explained is why you slept with me."

The truth choked her, and she knew she could never say it out loud to Jack. She loved him. It was that simple and that devastating. Ignoring what he asked, she said, "I agreed to do this for Alicia, because there wasn't a choice."

"Couldn't she have told Will about Lydia and gotten a police escort to the hospital?"

"She could have, but you've seen what the Terrines do. You know what they've done in the past, what they've tried to do this weekend. Do you think I could have lived with myself if I'd forced Alicia to get to Lydia through the police and then have the Terrine guns follow her?" She sat back, turning to look blindly out at the scattering of buildings on the side of the freeway. "You said yourself that there's a leak in the police, someone Terrine's used to get information."

"Will found the man." He glanced at her. "Do you remember Nicholes?"

"The man in the Hawaiian shirt?"

"That's the one. He tripped himself up, and Will's got him in custody. He was offered a deal, and he told Will everything. But he doesn't have a clue about what Terrine will order next."

"If Terrine could get a cop to turn, he could do just about anything. What would you have done if you'd been in my position?"

Jack was silent for a long while, and Ali faced him again. He was staring straight ahead, his hands gripping the steering wheel. "Well?" she asked.

Jack couldn't argue with the logic of what she'd done, but that didn't change the fact that it hurt like hell to be used. He'd never experienced a pain like he felt now, a dull ache that didn't diminish with time. And maybe the capper was that the case against Mick Terrine could very well be sliding down the river right now. If anyone deserved to rot in jail, it was Terrine. Right in the cell next to his father.

As he checked the rearview mirror, Jack saw a car swing in behind them. A sedan in an innocuous beige with two men in it. He held his breath until he saw the headlights flash once, then he looked to the right and the left. Two more cars came up on either side, nothing special about them, either, except the men driving—Stewart and Paven.

"Our escorts," Jack said, motioning vaguely around them. "And it's time for you to hit the floor."

She hesitated, and he felt his anger growing, partly anger at himself, partly anger at life in general and mostly anger at Ali. "Get down, now!" he bit out. "I thought you'd learned that lesson."

She moved quickly, crouching on the floor in front of the seat, and he could feel her staring at him. "You never answered my question," she said in a small voice.

He knew he shouldn't, but he looked at her. The instant he met her wide-eyed gaze, he knew there were questions he'd never be able to answer. To hell with what she'd asked. He said something he'd barely even thought through. "If *you* come out of that rest room and not your sister, you're going to be arrested. Conspiracy, fraud, criminal intent, accessory. You name it, you'll have it thrown at you."

He saw the way her face tightened, and he hated himself for what he was doing. He looked away, and saw the two cars at the side move up to cut in front of him and lead the way off the freeway. They eased through the stop sign and kept going in the direction of the courthouse.

Jack scanned the street as he made his way down it, seeing spotters here and there, cops posted to keep things clear. And he knew Will had done his job well.

"Well, would you have?" Ali persisted.

"Damn it, that isn't what's important here," he growled, not taking his eyes off the road. "You did it. You're responsible. That's the bottom line."

"Is it?" she said. "Isn't the bottom line that you might not have your revenge? That for five years you've wanted Mick Terrine to get what he deserves, and now it might not happen? Isn't that what makes you furious?"

The fact that she spoke a truth he'd barely been able to admit to only made him angrier. He glanced at her again, narrowing his eyes to blur her image. "Shut up and be ready to move when I tell you to."

She did as he said, and that only bothered Jack more. The silence in the car was deafening. He followed his escorts into the back parking lot of the courthouse and toward the secured entrance, and he found himself saying a silent prayer that Alicia Sullivan would be where she'd promised to be.

He slowed, turned the car so his door would be close to the entrance, then stopped behind the escort cars. The door to the courthouse was no more than twenty feet away. Just twenty feet more and they'd be inside, out of danger and moments from having this thing finished.

He flipped off the ignition, then looked at Ali. Her eyes were wide with fear and uncertainty, but she wasn't moving. She just watched him, waiting for him to give her the signal. God, she trusted him. After everything that had been said, she trusted him. In some way, that hurt him even more.

He looked away, saw the bodyguards were in position, then he said, "Follow me right now." He opened the door, pushed it back and got out. Using his body as a shield for Ali, he reached in and took her hand, helping her slide across the seat and step out into the heat and sun of the Monday morning.

Her fingers curled around his hand so tightly it made his skin tingle and his heart wrench. In that instant he knew the answer to her question. He would have done for his brothers exactly what she did for her sister. And damn the consequences.

As he turned to go inside, to put an end to the Terrines in his life, he heard a sound and saw a sight that shook him to his soul. A shot rang out on the hot air, then he saw Ali turn, as if in slow motion. Her mouth formed an "O" of surprise, her shirt flared at her shoulder. Shock and fear tore through him as he hurled himself at her. She'd been shot.

Chapter 13

In that moment, Ali's world was reduced to noise, fear and a blur of activity. Ali heard a cracking explosion, then another, and as she turned to Jack, she felt something whack her shoulder and send her spinning to one side. The next thing she knew, Jack was over her, pushing her flat onto the pavement of the parking lot, the heat and weight of his body encompassing her and protecting her.

Then Jack moved away from her, and as she twisted to see what was going on, the scene in front of her was frozen in mid-motion. What looked like an army of police stood with guns drawn, but all she saw was Jack. His gun free of the holster, aimed upward and fire flared from the barrel. She heard a scream.

She twisted and saw two men on the low roof of a service garage across the parking lot. She instantly

recognized one of the two men who had been following them as Benny. She'd never seen the other one.
Benny pitched forward, landing awkwardly on an
overhang above the garage doors. The other man, a
thin, dark-skinned man, stood up straight, a bright red
stain spreading at his stomach on the dead white of his
shirt. Then he clutched his middle. An expression of
complete surprise was stamped on his face as he tumbled forward off the roof and landed facedown on the
pavement.

In the next heartbeat, Ali was jerked to her feet and
dragged into the coolness of the courthouse. The door
swung shut, and the world of confusion and violence
was shut out, only to be replaced by more police who
formed a human shield around her and Jack. Guns
were pulled and held barrels down at the uniformed
officers' sides.

She looked at Jack, his face pale, and he just stared
at her. His breathing as rapid and uneven as her own,
he touched her cheek with unsteady fingers. The brush
of heat on her cold cheek unnerved her, but not as
much as the horror on Jack's face when his gaze
moved to her shoulder.

She looked down at her shirt and saw a hole in the
white cotton near the cap of her shoulder. She didn't
have to be told it was a bullet hole, but she didn't feel
any pain. Before she could do or say anything, Jack
quickly undid the three or four buttons and tugged the
cotton back to expose her shoulder.

His harshly exhaled breath echoed her own relief
when she saw that her skin had a red welt and bruise,
just about the same place as Jack had his scar, but

there wasn't any blood. His fingers skimmed over her skin, across the welt, as if to make sure he wasn't seeing things. Then his blue eyes lifted to her face again, and her world began to recede. The next thing she knew, Jack was muttering something about "killing all the bastards" and holding her tightly against his heart.

She understood one thing in that moment. This was right where she wanted to be, to feel his heat and strength supporting her. And she let herself lean on him, allowing him to be her anchor in this insanity. If only for this moment, she wanted to be lost in his embrace.

Jack knew that if he lived a million lifetimes, he would never forget that moment when he thought Ali had been shot, or his relief when he saw the rip in her shirt and only a dark welt on her pale skin. Fear had ripped through him. But not the fear he'd felt when he faced a felon, not the fear he'd felt when he'd faced Mick Terrine. This fear had been a living, horrible thing. As intense as his relief when he'd realized Ali was safe.

His instincts had taken over, and before he'd fully realized what was happening, both of Terrine's hired guns were facedown. The action had been born out of his training and his anger. And his need to protect this woman with every atom of his being.

Now, holding her, feeling her every breath, her breasts pressed to his chest, her head resting trustingly in the hollow of his shoulder, he had all his answers. No matter who he'd thought Ali was, what he thought she might have been or what she'd done, he loved her. And what a hell of a time to finally see the truth.

Will came back through the outer doors. "What happened back there?" Jack demanded in a tight voice.

"They slipped past my men. That roof was checked out five minutes before you came in. They knew how to get up there." Will grimaced with distaste. "A holdover from the Nicholes mess. And those men weren't about to tell us how they got there. You took them both out."

"Bastards," Jack muttered.

"And you're on leave again, as of now. Internal Affairs will probably investigate, but it's open and shut."

"I wasn't planning to hang around, anyway," Jack said.

"Then everyone's better for this." He looked at Ali, who was holding on to Jack, her face buried in his chest. "No one got hurt?"

Jack shook his head. "No, not really."

"Miss Sullivan, it's almost time to go inside." When Will spoke to her, Jack felt her tense. "Are you going to be all right?"

Slowly she eased back, and Jack hated losing her closeness. "I...I need to...to clean up a bit, if I can," she said in an unsteady voice, her eyes not meeting Jack's.

"Sure," Will said, then turned to one of the uniformed officers. "Check the ladies' room and see if it's clear."

Jack couldn't pull Ali back into his arms, but he could clear the way for her. "Let me do it," he said. "Just watch her, Will." Without looking back at Ali, he strode toward the rest room. *Be there, Alicia Sullivan,* he pleaded silently. *Be there.*

His hand hit the cold wood of the door, and he pushed it back to step inside.

The room, a long space, with a floor of pink marble, white-walled cubicles on one side and a long vanity with several sinks on the other, seemed empty. It *felt* empty. And Jack could feel his heart sink. What a hell of a mess this was going to be if Alicia Sullivan had chosen not to come back. He stooped down to look under the cubicle doors, saw nothing, then stood and waited a moment before he walked out. He'd never asked Ali how she and Alicia had made the switch before, and he just prayed that they had it covered this time.

He stepped back into the corridor where a ring of cops surrounded Ali. He gave a thumbs-up. "All clear."

A cop came in and handed Ali her purse, which she must have left in the car, then Will walked with her to where Jack stood by the door. "We've got an hour before they begin," he said to Ali. "But we need to do some preliminary work before going in. I can give you fifteen minutes. All right?"

She nodded. "Fifteen minutes." For one heart-stopping moment her green eyes met Jack's blue ones. And he would have given everything he owned to know what she was thinking. But loving someone didn't make him a mind reader. He didn't know what to say or do before she silently slipped into the room.

Ali went into the cold marble room and for a moment felt as if she was the last person on earth. Holding her purse with both hands, she slowly went to the end cubicle and pushed open the door. Ali didn't realize until that moment that she hadn't been entirely convinced Alicia would be here. There had been that niggling doubt bred from all those times Alicia had chosen to run instead of facing reality.

But as the door swung back with a softly protesting creak and thudded against the side wall, Ali saw her sister.

Alicia sat perched on the tank of the toilet, the baseball cap covering her curls. She was wearing the jeans, oversize sweatshirt and the deck shoes she'd taken from Ali on Friday. She just smiled at Ali, then scrambled off the toilet tank. When she saw Ali's shirt, her green eyes widened. She reached out and touched the fabric where the bullet had ripped it.

"What happened to you?" she asked in a whisper.

"They tried to kill me . . . kill you. Someone shot at me when we were coming into the courthouse."

"Oh, my God," Alicia breathed, and drew her hand back. "You . . . you've been shot?"

Ali tried to smile, but the expression wouldn't come for her. "No, I'm all right. It just grazed me."

Alicia tried to speak, but nothing came. Abruptly she pulled Ali to her, and the sisters clung to each other for a long moment. "I swear I didn't know anything like that could happen," she whispered. "Mick's crazy, but I didn't ever think . . ."

She hugged Ali even tighter, then stood back. "I thought they could use you or Lydia, maybe threaten you to put pressure on me . . ." Her eyes darted back to the bullet hole. "I never, never thought . . ." She tried to smile, but made a weak expression at best. "But you're okay, and that's what counts, isn't it?"

"Well, it's over," Ali said. "But you have to get into the grand-jury room, and we need to change clothes." She began to unbutton her top. "You saw Lydia, didn't you?"

"Yes, and she knew it was me right away," Alicia said as she began to strip. "I never could fool her." She unzipped her jeans and pushed them down over her hips. "She knows about everything, and she wasn't really surprised. I thought it would upset her, but she was so calm. It sort of reminded me of that fiasco with Brad ten years ago."

This wasn't exactly like that night, but there were similarities. Ali taking the blame for Alicia. Ali hating what she'd done, but never able to say no to Alicia. And Lydia always understanding Alicia, but Alicia never really knowing she would until it was too late. "And she's doing all right?" Ali asked as she took the jeans from Alicia.

"She's great." Alicia pulled on the ruined shirt and grimaced at the tear in the shoulder. "God, that was close."

"Too close," Ali agreed, then, as she put on Alicia's jeans and zipped them, she looked at her sister. "How close were you to Mick Terrine?"

Her sister kept dressing. "He'd come by the blackjack table, then he asked me out a couple of times. That night I was supposed to meet him in the casino, but he called and said he had to do some business and he asked if I'd meet him in the parking lot of the hotel." She buttoned the shirt, not looking at Ali as she worked. "He was dead drunk, and I helped him up to his room. He talked and talked and talked, then threw up and passed out.''

"You never went to bed with him?"

Alicia looked at Ali and grimaced. "No, never. I wouldn't." She pulled off her cap, and as the curls tumbled around her shoulders, she handed it to Ali. "And I never would have, either."

Ali twisted her hair up and off her neck, then pulled the cap down over it. "What are you going to do now?"

Alicia sat on the closed lid of the toilet and tugged on the shoes Ali gave her. As she did up the laces, she looked up at her sister. "I'll tell them what they need to know about Mick that night, then decide about going into the Witness Protection Program."

Ali stopped in the middle of putting on the deck shoes. "I thought they said you'd refused to do that."

"I did, but I think that's what I'll have to do. I can't pull you and Lydia into this any further." She shrugged and stood. "Go figure. I finally get it straight in my mind that family and roots are everything, and I'll have to be on my own." She raked at her hair with her fingers. "Maybe I've finally grown up."

Maybe they both had this weekend. Ali knew she'd changed in the most fundamental way. But it shocked her to hear Alicia, the person who'd left home so she wouldn't be confined, who never stopped moving, to say she was willing to let someone else control her life.

"I'm going to stay around until I make sure you get through this," Ali said, prouder of her sister than she could ever remember being before.

Alicia shook her head. "Oh, no, you won't. Lydia needs you, and I can't stand the thought of anyone seeing you and putting two and two together." Alicia fluffed her hair some more and frowned. "I can't be responsible for anyone else getting hurt."

"Alicia, the Terrines could still kill you. You might testify and send that jerk away, but do you think they're going to send you a thank-you note and invite you up for tea?" That sounded so much like Jack's words that it stopped her.

"I'll deal with that. But you and Lydia won't have to." She hugged Ali so tightly she could barely breathe, then stood back. "At least you had a nice calm weekend at a fancy hotel."

"Sure," Ali murmured.

Alicia smoothed the damaged shirt, then managed a weak smile. "Don't look so worried. This weekend's over. Forget about it."

How could she ever forget that in a few short days she'd found out what it was to love someone and what it was to lose that love? That thought made her heart lurch.

"Hey," Alicia was saying, "it's my problem, and it's going to be fine. Lydia's going to do all right, and I'll take care of things. You take care of your own life, and I promise you won't have to pick up the pieces of mine ever again."

She just had to pick up the pieces of her own life, Ali thought. "I love you," Ali whispered.

"Me, too," Alicia said, then slipped out of the stall and headed for the door.

Jack saw the door to the rest room open, and the next instant he saw the tumble of brilliant hair, long legs, a tear burned in the upper shoulder of the shirt, soiled jeans and scuffed shoes. Ali. His heart dropped, but then he found himself looking into the green eyes of a stranger.

Alicia was back, and his relief left him light-headed.

The beauty was the same, the stunning brilliance of her hair, the delicate bones, the leggy figure, but there was something so basically different about the two women that he knew he would never have been fooled by Ali's charade if he had known Alicia first. It must be that loving someone made them special to you.

He stared at Alicia as Will spoke quickly to her. Love. That word settled in his soul. When they were shooting at Ali, he knew then that she was more important to him than anything. He must have loved her from the start, but he'd been too blind, too caught up in his grudge against Mick Terrine and too caught up in this business to realize it until today.

Alicia looked at him briefly, not recognizing him at all, then past him to Will. "Are you ready to get this over with?" she asked. Even her voice was a shade different from Ali's.

But Will didn't act as if he heard or saw anything different. He came up to Alicia, took her by her upper arm, then turned to look at Jack. "Are you coming along to see the show?"

Jack shook his head. "No, I've gone far enough with this."

Will didn't argue. "Let's go," he said, then started off with Alicia, the uniformed officers closing around them like a blanket.

Jack stood alone in the corridor as the group disappeared around the corner. Then as the sounds faded away, he turned and stared at the door to the rest room.

He wanted Ali to come out. He wanted Ali to look at him, and Ali was the one he wanted to hold on to and tell that he loved her. No matter who she was or what she did. But the door didn't move. He waited for more than ten minutes, then he moved closer, but couldn't hear anything inside. He rapped on the wood, waited, but there wasn't any response.

He spotted a private security guard near the doors to one of the offices down the way and hurried over to him. "Excuse me," he said, taking out his badge and flipping it over for the man. "I need your help."

The guard, a pale-skinned kid who looked barely old enough to shave, looked at him, then read his badge. "What do you need?"

"I need you to come with me for a minute," Jack said as he pushed his badge into his back pocket.

"I don't know. I'm supposed to be watching these offices."

"Good. You can still keep an eye on them and help me out." Jack pulled out his wallet, took out his last ten dollars and tucked it into the top pocket of the kid's uniform. "It would really help me out."

The kid patted his pocket. "As long as I can do my job I don't see any reason we both can't benefit."

"I knew you'd see it my way," Jack said, and led the way to the rest-room door. "All you have to do is stay here, and don't let anyone in here for any reason."

The kid stopped by Jack and looked at the door with the gold plaque that said Women. Jack had to hand it to him. He could see the suggestion of a smile, but all the kid did was move to one side of the doors and lean against the wall. "You can trust me to keep everyone out of there, sir."

"Thanks," Jack murmured, then went inside.

He let the door close behind him, and then stood very still. When he'd come in here before, it had felt empty, but now he knew it wasn't. He could literally feel the presence of Ali, even though he couldn't see her. He moved farther into the room, then stopped by the row of sinks and mirror.

"Ali?" he said, his voice soft, yet echoing back to him off the cold marble.

There was nothing for a moment, then the door at the end cubicle slowly opened and Ali stepped out. Her hair was confined by an old baseball cap, and her clothes were oversize and loose. She looked like a waif.

He took a step toward her and could tell she'd been crying. Her lashes were wet spikes, and moisture still lingered on her pale cheeks.

"What are you doing in here?" she asked, staying by the cubicle door.

"Alicia came back," he said.

"I told you she would." She wrapped her arms around herself. "She'll be safe, won't she?"

He didn't move. "Will's protecting her. He'll make sure she'll be all right."

"I think she's decided to go into the Witness Protection Program."

"That might be for the best," he said, the words filling the space that separated him from Ali.

"She'll be all alone," Ali whispered, her bottom lip suddenly unsteady.

"She'll have a new life and be safe."

"You don't understand." She moved to the counter and touched it with one hand. "We were alone most of our lives, until we were sent to Lydia's. Then we were a family for a while. Even though Alicia took off after graduation, she could always come back. I always knew she was there." Ali tossed her purse onto the counter and turned to face the mirror.

She stared at herself for a long moment. "Two halves of a whole, two parts of a soul." She shook her head. "Someone told me that. I don't remember who. Maybe one of the social workers who let Alicia and me be in the same foster home." She looked at him, her eyes brilliant with the threat of fresh tears. "She's all I have. And she'll be gone."

Jack moved closer to Ali. "She's not all you have."

She looked away from him, her head bowing. "You're right. There's Lydia. God knows she's just like a mother. I really do love her."

"That's why you were willing to take Alicia's place this weekend. You love Lydia and you love your sister."

"And I'd do it again, even if it meant I'd get shot at twice, be forced to run halfway across Nevada, ride with smelly sheep, and . . ." Her voice trailed off.

"We survived."

She glanced at him, her eyes narrowed, as if she couldn't quite look at him directly. "Did we?" she whispered.

"I asked you a question in the car."

"What question?" she asked, her voice flat.

"Why did you sleep with me?"

She turned away from him and turned on the tap, then cupped water in her hands and splashed her face.

While she blotted her face with a paper towel, the room was silent.

Then Jack spoke up. "Ali?"

She turned and looked at him as she tossed the paper towel into the trash bin. "What do you want from me, Jack?"

"The truth."

Ali could barely look at him. The light in the room was bright and unkind in some respects, making his image in front of her so clear it hurt. At the same time, it gave her a lot to remember. The way his hair lay at his temples, the way he had of partially squinting when he was intent on what was happening around him and the way he fingered the scar on his chin when he was nervous. "What truth?" she asked.

He came closer, and he stirred the air around her, filling her senses with his essence. Not fair, damn it. But then life had never been fair to her. She turned to look in the mirror, at a woman with a face tinged with paleness and etched with tension. What difference would it make now to tell him the truth? All she had to do was say the words, then walk out of here and never look back.

She saw him in the mirror, not more than two feet from her. She saw him reach out, his hand touch her shoulder, and she didn't move. His heat seared her through her sweatshirt, but she endured it. One more thing to take with her when she walked out.

His blue eyes met hers in the mirror. "All I want is the truth, Ali. That's all I ever wanted."

"And all I gave you was lies, wasn't it?"

"Was it?"

"Mostly," she admitted. But she couldn't let him believe that what she'd offered him had been a lie.

"Ali—?" His hand on her shoulder tightened, and she jerked back, unable to take it any longer.

There was no more whispering, no soft tones. The words exploded from her. "What do you want from me? Mick Terrine's going to rot in prison. That's what you wanted, isn't it? That's why you agreed to watch me, why you made sure I got back here in one piece."

He stared down at her. "I want Mick Terrine to be out of circulation for good, that's true. But there's something I want even more. Something I didn't even know I wanted, until recently."

"To pass that damned exam?"

"That, too. Believe me, I've sweated blood for the chance, and I'll do it." She hated him when he reached out to her again, capturing her chin in one strong hand. She could get free at any moment. She knew that, yet she knew that she'd never be free of this man. And she knew she could hate him for that.

She looked down, not able to meet his penetrating gaze. "You know you're in the ladies' room, don't you?" she muttered.

"Ask me *why* I'm here in this pink marble palace."

Her gaze lifted to meet his. "What?"

"Repeat after me, 'Why are you in the ladies' room, Jack?'"

She stared at him.

"Repeat that," he insisted softly.

"Why... why are you here?" she finally managed.

"Good. You can still follow directions—sort of." A shadow of a smile flitted at the corners of his mouth, giving her the most irrational desire to touch her lips to it to see if it would give her a smile in return.

"Why are you here?" she asked again.

His mouth softened even more. "I'm here because I love you."

This room was playing havoc with the acoustics, the echoes making words born out of her imagination, not out of reality. "What?" she asked.

"I love you, Alison..." He frowned. "Do you have a middle name?"

"Carole," she whispered.

"Good, I like that. I love you, Alison Carole Sullivan."

And her smile came. One of wonder and joy. Miracles did happen. And she was standing smack dab in the middle of the biggest miracle she'd ever heard of. "You love me?"

"Only if you love me," he said seriously.

In one stroke, her world was as close to perfect as she knew it would ever be. "I love you, I do," she said, and the next thing she knew she was in his arms. His lips found hers, and Ali knew the true meaning of happiness.

"Excuse me," someone said from behind them.

Jack framed her face with his hands and moved back, but his eyes never left her face. "What is it?"

"There's a lot of excitement going on down the hall. I can't stay out here any longer. I've got to get back to my post."

Alicia. Something had happened to her. Ali felt her happiness start to slip out of her grasp, even though Jack still held her, anchoring her, grounding her. "What's going on?" Jack asked without turning.

"The word is Mick Terrine's dead."

Chapter 14

Jack took Ali by the hand and hurried out of the rest room, almost running into Will coming down the corridor. Will stopped dead in his tracks, glanced behind him, then moved toward Ali, looking for all the world as if he'd seen a ghost. "How did you—"

Jack cut in. "What's going on with Terrine?"

Will moved to one side to let some cops rush past, heading for the front of the courthouse, but he didn't stop staring at Ali. "What in the hell's going on *here?* How did you get back here? You're supposed to be under guard." He looked at her hat and clothes, then back to her. "And how did you get into those clothes?"

Jack put his arm around Ali's shoulder, hugging her to his side. "This is Alison Sullivan, Alicia's twin, her mirror twin. I'll explain it all later. Just tell me what's going on with Terrine."

Will blinked, then looked at Jack. "He's dead. They found him ten minutes ago in his cell."

Jack's hold on Ali tightened with each word Will uttered. "He killed himself?"

"They thought so at first, then Sharp—you know, that bald guy that works for the old man?—was found where he shouldn't be. He had a syringe in his pocket. It looks as if he offed the kid."

Ali held on to Jack for dear life. "His father ordered it, didn't he?" she said.

"It looks that way."

"Ugly people," Jack murmured.

"My sister?" Ali asked. "Is she all right?"

"We'll have to hold her for a while until we untangle this mess, but she'll be fine." He stared at Ali. "You're her identical twin?"

"Almost identical," Jack said.

"I'll be damned," Will muttered.

"No, I think Mick Terrine will be." He exhaled. "And if there's any justice, so will his father. I don't suppose Sharp is talking?"

"I'm not counting on it. That guy would go through fire for the old man." He looked at Ali, then back to Jack. "You *will* explain all this to me later, won't you?"

"As soon as I figure it out," Jack assured him.

"Oh, by the way," Will said, "I got this crazy call from some guy named Crane. He said to tell you he did the best he could, and he hoped he gave you enough time to get in."

"Crane called you?" Ali asked.

"Just a few minutes before you got here. He called the house and gave my wife the message. She didn't know what it meant, so she had it radioed in. What was that all about?''

"I'll explain that, too."

"I hope you can." Will looked at Ali again, then turned and went back down the hall.

Ali watched him go, then said to Jack, "What's going to happen to my sister now?"

"If Terrine really had his own son killed to keep him quiet, I'd say it's a wash. There'd be no point in his taking out Alicia. The old man will be busy enough distancing himself from it. He won't want to draw any more attention to himself."

"How could he have hated his son enough to kill him?" she asked, horrified.

"I told you when we talked about this before, he didn't hate him. He just knew that Mick was weak, and a weak person is always a liability, especially to an organization like Terrine's. George must have had it set that if Alicia got to the grand jury, Junior had to go. He knew the D.A. would try to work a deal, and Mick probably would have taken it, instead of a first-degree murder charge. That probably scared him as much as anything could in this life."

His eyes were intense, and there were heavy brackets around his mouth. "And you're angry that Mick Terrine slipped past what you think he deserved, aren't you?" Ali said.

"No trial, no justice."

"Being dead is a long time," Ali pointed out.

"You're right." He pulled her over to the wall and out of the way of the people who were hurrying to the back section of the courthouse. "Forever is a long, long time."

"Forever." She smiled as the pressures of the weekend began lifting.

"And how do you feel about a life sentence?" he asked.

"I don't know anything about the law. I don't—"

"For you," he said, his expression easing into a slow smile that made her heart jump.

"A life sentence?"

"Forever."

She went into his arms. "You're going to make a terrific lawyer," she said, her voice muffled against his chest. "You can make a life sentence sound like paradise."

One week later—Los Angeles

The twins came out of the hospital room, and Jack watched them strip off the hospital gowns, give them to a nurse at the desk of the cardiac unit. Then both of them turned and saw him. They hurried down the green-tile corridor, and for a moment, Jack saw two of a kind, identical sisters, exhausted from their vigil by Lydia's bed, both pale and weary.

But as they came toward him, he knew Ali was the one on the left. It wasn't because of the different clothes, Ali in mussed beige slacks and white sweater, and Alicia in jeans and a tie-dyed T-shirt. He would have known if they'd been in identical clothes. And he held out his arms to Ali. As she slipped into his embrace, he doubted he would ever get used to the feeling of holding her, of having his whole being respond to her and ache with love for her.

He held her tightly, inhaling her sweetness and relishing the feel of her so close to him. As he slowly stroked her back, he rested his chin on her curls and looked over at Alicia, standing a few feet away watching them.

Ali had been crying, but now she was smiling. "Lydia's going to be fine. The infection's completely under control, and the doctor said she'll be out of isolation tomorrow."

Jack felt great relief, as much for Ali as he did for Lydia, a lady he had yet to meet. The operation had been hard on Ali. Long hours of waiting and hoping, then three days when there'd been an infection and Ali had refused to leave the hospital. It had all taken a toll.

"She wants to meet you tomorrow," Ali said, hugging him tightly for a moment before she moved back just enough to see into his face.

"I hope I pass the test."

"With flying colors," she murmured.

"Heck, Lydia will take one look at you and know in a second if you're for real or not," Alicia said.

"Oh, I'm for real," Jack whispered for Ali's ears only. He saw the glow in her eyes, a fire that was pushing back the weariness there. He dropped a kiss on her lips. The contact was fleeting, but it created enough heat to make his breath catch. "You need sleep."

"She sure does," Alicia said. "Why don't you get her to do that very thing, and I'll stay with Lydia for a while?"

Jack didn't look away from Ali, his arms loosely around her shoulders. "Will you come to the room for some rest?"

She nodded, her tongue touching her pale lips. "As long as you come with me."

"Why, sister," Alicia said. "I do believe you're propositioning this poor man."

Jack smiled at Ali, watching the color rise in her cheeks. "I do believe you need a shower and a change of clothes. Why don't you take care of that, and—" she looked back up at Jack and her smile came, slow and easy, the first smile in what seemed like an eternity to Jack "—I'll take care of myself."

"I believe you will," Alicia said. "I'm going back in with Lydia for a while, then I'll go to the house and pick up some fresh clothes for both of us."

Ali nodded. "Good. That sounds fine. When you get back—"

"I'll know where to find you," Alicia said, then, "And Mr. Graham, you're welcome to this family as long as you treat my sister right."

"I'll make it my life's project," Jack murmured.

"I just bet you will," Alicia said. "I'm leaving now."

Ali and Jack both said goodbye.

Alicia laughed, a light welcome sound in the sterile confines of the cardiac unit. "See you later," she said, and walked away.

Ali waited until Alicia had gone, then she swallowed hard, her feelings raw and brilliant at that moment. "Did I tell you today that I love you?" she whispered.

"I'm not sure. Say it again, just in case you didn't."

"I love you, Jack Graham."

She barely got the words out before Jack turned, taking her by her hand and leading her down the corridor. Jack had taken care of everything since they'd returned to Los Angeles. He'd dealt with doctors who talked double talk, got Ali and Alicia in to see Lydia when she wasn't supposed to have visitors, and he'd managed to get a room for them on the same floor where Lydia was being treated.

But Ali hadn't spent much time in the room. And when she'd been in there, she'd paced and worried. Now Jack was taking her to the room. He pushed back the door and pulled her in with him. A single lamp by one of the two beds was on, and Ali was shocked to see the night through the windows. She'd lost track of time.

She glanced at the clock on the nightstand. Midnight.

Jack crossed to the bed and took a scattering of law books off it, stacking them on the floor. Then he came back for Ali. He framed her face with his hands.

"How are you doing?"

"I'm making it." She glanced at the stacked books. "But you didn't get to take the exam."

"I'm going to take it, but not in Nevada. I'll take it here, in California."

"What?"

"You don't want to live in Nevada, do you?"

"No, but—"

"Neither do I. I didn't find you just to have you living in California and me practicing law in Nevada. I looked into taking the California exam, and I've got plenty of time to study for it."

"Are you sure?"

"Very sure. Oh, I talked to Crane. He got his phone reconnected, and he says to tell you that he's glad you made it."

"He sure took a chance letting us stay there," Ali said.

"Yeah, he did. I sent him a thank-you gift—a case of the best whiskey I could find."

She laughed, the sound unsteady but genuine. "Are you going to go back there and drink it with him?"

"Maybe later, but not now." His thumbs moved slowly across her cheeks. "Right now it's my job to see that you get some rest. You need to recharge."

"I need you," she said simply, the truth sweet on her tongue.

He slid one hand under her curls, cupping the nape of her neck. "In a hospital?"

"Life and death," she whispered, knowing that was the magnitude of her need for this man. "They deal with it all the time." She slipped away from him and crossed to the door. With a flick of her wrist, the door was locked, and she turned back to Jack. "You promised my sister that you'd treat me right."

"Yes, I did, didn't I?"

She came back to him, but didn't touch him. "What's your definition of treating me right?"

He smiled, a seductive expression that made Ali feel a hunger for this man she knew would never be satisfied. Without a word he swept her into his arms and carried her to the bed, then sat down with her on the edge. "Let me *show* you my definition."

"Oh, yes, do," she breathed, her arms draping around his neck and drawing him to her.

The kiss was quick and fierce, then Ali was in Jack's arms. She ran her hands over his shoulders and arms, needing to feel him, but hating the barrier of clothes between them. As if he read her mind, Jack tugged her sweater up and over her head. He tossed it aside, not caring where it landed, then his fingers found the zipper of her slacks.

Ali never would remember exactly how it happened, but in what seemed a single heartbeat, she and Jack were together in the bed with nothing between them. His heat was hers, his heartbeat an echo of her own. And to say she felt as if she belonged where she was was truly the understatement of the year. She not only felt as if she belonged, but when Jack's hands explored her, and his lips tasted her, she knew she'd been waiting for this moment all her life.

She went to him, felt him, touched him, stroked him, loved him. She loved him completely and honestly, and when they fused into one soul, when the world disappeared and left them as one, she knew she would never be alone again.

And later, as Ali held Jack, snuggling into his side, she was satisfied for the moment but certain that the hunger would come again, and again, and again. And she welcomed the idea.

Jack reached out and flicked the privacy curtain along its stock. The white material almost circled the bed, shutting out the rest of the room. "Walls of Jericho," he murmured.

"And we're both on the same side," Ali whispered.

He drew her tightly to his side, his lips brushing her forehead, and he whispered, "So, Alison Carole Sullivan, did I treat you right?"

She shifted and looked down at him, then pressed her lips to the scar on his shoulder. "I'm not sure," she murmured against the heat of his skin. "Don't you think we should go through that again?"

He laughed, then pulled her back to him. "Gladly!"

* * * * *

For all those readers who've been looking for something a little bit different, a little bit spooky, let Silhouette Books take you on a journey to the dark side of love with

SILHOUETTE Shadows™

If you like your romance mixed with a hint of danger, a taste of something eerie and wild, you'll love Shadows. This new line will send a shiver down your spine and make your heart beat faster. It's full of romance and more—and some of your favorite authors will be featured right from the start. Look for our four launch titles wherever books are sold, because you won't want to miss a single one.

THE LAST CAVALIER—Heather Graham Pozzessere
WHO IS DEBORAH?—Elise Title
STRANGER IN THE MIST—Lee Karr
SWAMP SECRETS—Carla Cassidy

After that, look for two books every month, and prepare to tremble with fear—and passion.

SILHOUETTE SHADOWS, coming your way in March.

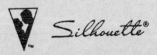

Silhouette®

SHAD1

Take 4 bestselling love stories FREE

Plus get a FREE surprise gift!

Silhouette Intimate Moments
is proud to present
Mary Anne Wilson's
SISTER, SISTER duet—
Two halves of a whole,
two parts of a soul

In the mirror, Alicia and Alison Sullivan both had brilliant red hair and green eyes—but in personality and life-style, these identical twins were as different as night and day. Alison needed control, order and stability. Alicia, on the other hand, hated constraints, and the idea of settling down bored her.

Despite their differences, they had one thing in common—a need to be loved and cherished by a special man. And to fulfill their goals, these two sisters would do anything for each other—including switching places in a life-threatening situation.

Look for Alison and Jack's adventure in TWO FOR THE ROAD (IM #472, January 1993), and Alicia and Steven's story in TWO AGAINST THE WORLD (IM #489, April 1993)—and *enjoy!*

SISTERR

▼INTIMATE MOMENTS®
™ *Silhouette* ®